"I'm too heavy. I'll pull us both in!"

"I've got it fastened around the axle of your truck."

"Dory..."

"Do it right now, Chad Dooley Jaggert!"

Her shriek and the use of his full name punched through his pain. With one hand he managed to grab the rope. His numb fingers struggled against the nylon.

"Hurry." Dory's voice was pitched high with panic.

"I've almost done it. Get back to the truck," he called to her.

Once he got the rope fastened, she could haul him up quickly using the truck. Dory straightened suddenly, as if she'd heard something. He saw her knuckles whiten on the railing.

"What is it?" he hollered over the wind.

And then he felt it, too, the undulation of the bridge, the wood uncoiling like some giant snake. Too late.

"Run, Dory!"

He did not know if she heard him or not.

With a spine-shivering moan the bridge collapsed. The rope slithered from his hands.

As he pinwheeled into the darkness, he watched in helpless horror as Dory was thrown into the void alongside him.

Dana Mentink is a national bestselling author. She has been honored to win two Carol Awards, a HOLT Medallion and an RT Reviewers' Choice Best Book Award. She's authored more than thirty novels to date for Love Inspired Suspense and Harlequin Heartwarming. Dana loves feedback from her readers. Contact her at danamentink.com.

SECRETS
RESURFACED

DANA MENTINK

LOVE INSPIRED SUSPENSE
INSPIRATIONAL ROMANCE

LOVE INSPIRED SUSPENSE
INSPIRATIONAL ROMANCE

ISBN-13: 978-1-335-40286-8

Secrets Resurfaced

This is a work of fiction. Names, characters, places and incidents are either the product of the author's imagination or are used fictitiously. Any resemblance to actual persons, living or dead, businesses, companies, events or locales is entirely coincidental.

This edition published by arrangement with Harlequin Books S.A.

For questions and comments about the quality of this book, please contact us at CustomerService@Harlequin.com.

Love Inspired
22 Adelaide St. West, 40th Floor
Toronto, Ontario M5H 4E3, Canada
www.Harlequin.com

Printed in U.S.A.

Remember ye not the former things, neither consider the things of old. Behold, I will do a new thing; now it shall spring forth; shall ye not know it? I will even make a way in the wilderness, and rivers in the desert.

—Isaiah 43:18-19

To Grandma and Grandpa Mentink,
the perfect examples of selfless love and grace.

ONE

Show yourself.

Dory Winslow peered down into the darkening canyon, searching for her quarry in the lengthening shadows. Her muscles were cramped from crouching. Grit clung to her hair where it poked out from underneath her cap. If anyone saw her there, binoculars pressed to her eyes, face streaked with sweat from an unseasonably hot April, they might think she was a stalker. In a way, they'd be right. She lifted the binoculars, careful to angle them so the failing sunlight would not strike the lenses.

Rocks bit into her elbow where she squeezed against the granite shelf. Far below, the rising silver moonlight reflected off the ribbon of river that eventually meandered along to the ocean. She took in the twisted rock layers, jutting here and there, white and porous. It might as well have been a desert canyon. Odd that not two miles away from this desolate spot was the magnificent central coast of California, a place where ranch land butted up to the beach, a breathtaking patchwork of grassland and surf unlike any other.

The faintest saltwater freshness trickled across her

senses and reawakened the familiar sorrow. She could never picture the ocean without thinking of what she'd lost to it. Chad Jaggert, her life here in Driftwood, their future, all turned upside down by the voracious sea. She recalled the moment five years before when she'd heard the tragic news. Her father, a private investigator for the DA's office, had broken it to her as she'd returned from registering for her second semester of junior college classes. It had been exactly one month before her twentieth birthday.

Honey, Chad's father wrecked his boat and killed someone. It looks like the fool was drinking. He's under arrest.

Through the shock, she'd not missed the edge of satisfaction in her father's tone, as if the tragedy was a validation for what he'd told her since she'd started dating Chad.

He's no good for you. His family's a mess. You can do better than Chad Jaggert.

Her dad despised Rocky Jaggert, pure and simple. Their rift had started long before she and Chad had even met.

Her heart had split wide open in that moment for Chad and his father. But that had been only the beginning of the mess.

Now the rock walls seemed to squeeze in, punishing her for her decision to come back, even temporarily.

There's nothing for you here but pain, she could almost hear them whisper.

"And answers," she mumbled through gritted teeth. She wasn't leaving without those.

A scraping noise snapped her to attention. Was it the scuff of a boot on the rocks? Or the natural sounds of the wind and weather? Frozen, she watched and listened. A bat winged over the canyon top. She tried to ease the cramp in her legs without changing position, a skill she'd learned over her five-year span as a private investigator under her father's tutelage. Was the fugitive she sought finally within her sights? Had he heard her approach? Seen her Jeep parked in the dense cluster of forest that ringed the canyon?

She ignored her screaming muscles and stayed stone-still. Most of the time, stillness was more effective than running. It had been a hard-learned lesson. Her father had drilled three things into Dory's head. *Do your research. Call in the cops when appropriate. Collect your fee.* But there was one other rule she hadn't followed this time. *Always let someone know your location during a pursuit.*

Dory'd not told a single soul of her plans to return to Driftwood. It would be smart to send a text to her father now, to inform him of where she was in case things went wrong, but that would require explanations she was not prepared to give. Besides, she told herself, even if she'd wanted to, she probably wouldn't get a signal, she was tucked so deep in this twisted nowhere. She was on her own, as she had been since Chad had cut her out of his life. Her fingers found the silver heart locket.

No, not alone, she reminded herself.

This time she heard the unmistakable sound of movement from below. She focused the lenses, breath catching as she saw a hooded figure hiking along the stone-littered trail. She picked out the red glow of a cigarette.

Blaze was a smoker—that much she knew. All the other attributes appeared to fit her target, also. She pegged him at midtwenties, tall and skinny and… Was that a glimpse of dark red hair she caught from underneath the hood? A hefty pack weighed the guy down and he stopped to flick the ash off his cigarette. He had the comfortable gait of someone familiar with the terrain. A shiver went up her spine. Her info had been right. Blaze was holing up in the canyon. Why, she couldn't imagine, but now was not the time to speculate.

She eased out her cell phone to take a picture, but her elbow set a rock into motion. She froze.

"Someone there?" Blaze called.

She willed every nerve to quiet, every muscle to still.

After a moment, he took another drag on his cigarette and continued walking.

She let out a gusty breath at how close she'd come to blowing it. She had to get a photo first, to prove he was who she suspected. Then there would be time for questions.

She'd used every arsenal in her PI toolbox, but it hadn't been easy. Her quarry had not accessed an ATM or credit card that she was aware of. He'd given a fake name, Brian Upton, at the halfway house where he'd last stayed and ridden buses or thumbed rides instead of renting a car. But Dory was very good at what she did. She had the patience and tenacity. It paid her bills.

Only this time, she wasn't after a paycheck. This time, it was personal.

"I know who you really are," Dory whispered to herself. "And you're going to tell me the rest of your secrets, right here, right now."

Chad Jaggert handed the clipboard to his adopted brother, Liam, without a word. He'd come to know Liam when ranch owners Gus and Ginny hired Chad on to do some extra chores when his father was drinking away their food money. Liam didn't mind Chad's silent tendencies and they'd become closer than blood, as he had with another ranch hand, Mitch Whitehorse. Liam perused the clipboard. On it was a meticulous record of three thousand head of cattle, including the calves that would be kept with their mothers until the late summer weaning.

The springtime duties that had taken him over the sprawling property of Roughwater Ranch had been especially entertaining, thanks to the antics of the young calves and their reactions to Liam's goofy dog Jingles and his equally goofy companion Meatball. If those dogs ever learned to herd properly, Chad would swallow his hat.

His contentment at a day well spent on horseback had evaporated, however, when he'd returned to the corral and noted the agitation of their newest horse.

The gelding was pawing at the ground and pacing the fence line.

Most animals felt immediately better when joined with a herd. Family friend and horse breeder Tom Rourke warned before he'd delivered the horse that there could be some settling-in "issues." He'd rescued Boss from an abandoned farm where he'd been completely alone, so there was no telling how the horse was feeling about his abrupt change of circumstances.

Chad approached the fence. "Easy there, Boss."

Liam peered at Chad closely, dissecting him in that way only an ex–Green Beret could. "Problem?" Liam's North Carolina drawl misled people into thinking he was laid-back and easygoing. Not even close.

"Not sure," Chad said.

"Say again?"

It didn't matter that Liam was losing his hearing to otosclerosis. Liam would instinctively know that something was bothering Chad even if he couldn't hear a single syllable.

"Got our first veterans arriving next month, and I'm worried Boss might not be ready."

Aunt Ginny and Uncle Gus were graciously allowing Chad to start up the Horses for Heroes program at the Roughwater Ranch. Though Chad had never served, all his life he'd wanted to help those who had, especially those who lived with horrors that had changed them. His own father, Rocky, a retired Marine, would only speak of his time in Vietnam in short, reluctant bursts.

It was a great idea, rescued horses rescuing troubled vets. So why had he hit so many roadblocks? Red tape. Insurance issues. Now an unsettled horse. Detours. Why was he surprised? His life had been a series of them.

Liam pulled on his cowboy hat. "Gonna be dark soon. Let's take him out. Maybe some away time will do the trick."

"I'll do it," Chad said. "Maggie will be expecting you for dinner."

The mention of his new wife brought a smile to Liam's lips. "She's off tonight. We're gonna go into town for some supper at the Chuckwagon and she has threatened to drag me to the dance floor." He frowned. "But if you need me, I'll call her and—"

"Go."

"If you want a second opinion, maybe Mitch—"

"He has a T-ball meeting."

Their older brother had barely made it through his

ranch chores in time to hurry off to his wife, Jane, and adopted son, Charlie. Family time was precious to Mitch, each moment to be savored since he'd rescued Charlie from his biological father—Mitch's brother, a serial killer.

They'd all been working to fence off a pasture to accommodate the installation of the solar panels that would generate additional income for the ranch. The Roughwater, like every other ranch, was capital intensive and return deficient. Even with Liam's assistance and the help of Tom Rourke, Mitch had almost not completed the job in time to meet his family.

Liam had Maggie.

Mitch had Jane and Charlie.

His almost-sister Helen was enjoying her new life with Sergio and their twin girls after they'd almost been taken out during a cold-case investigation.

Life was settling into a peaceful lull. Seemed like everyone had someone to go home to. Chad had almost had that once, too. He shrugged away the ache. "I got this," he told Liam.

Liam hesitated for another moment. "Call if you need backup. You know I'll be there."

Chad decided that what Boss needed more than quiet time was a mentor. So he saddled his quarter horse Zephyr and led him out, leaving the gate open for Boss. He smoothed a hand over Zephyr's chocolate-brown side. If his instincts were correct, Boss would follow his quiet, confident mount and they'd get some air and return. If he was wrong, Boss would take off and Chad and Zephyr would spend the rest of the night trying to recapture him.

Though Chad was anxious to complete their out-ing before dark, he gave Boss all the time he needed. It was a small show of respect considering the horse's troubled past. When Boss eased up behind them, Chad guided Zephyr away from the ranch along the western trail that led off the property.

Tom Rourke called his cell. "Hey. Saw you going somewhere with Boss. What's up?"

"He's acting stressed. Taking him for a ride, is all."

Tom sighed. "I wasn't sure about bringing you that horse, but you know he's a beauty."

"And you're a sucker for a needy horse."

Tom laughed. "Guilty. Call if you need help."

Chad didn't think he would, but he'd learned everything about ranching was unpredictable. Too many opportunities for disaster on an enormous property that was home to thousands of adult cattle that tipped the scales at twelve hundred pounds. The herd was not accustomed to a lot of human contact, except for that of the ranch hands.

He and Zephyr set a brisk pace. The horse's nostrils flared as he sampled the early evening air. Boss appeared to relax. Perhaps he was like Chad. They both relished their quiet time.

Passing through the gate, Chad locked it behind them and they continued on.

The grassy trail gradually sloped until they reached a spot where they could view the lower rim of the canyon. He reined Zephyr to a halt as a distant gleam caught his eye. He noted a car tucked deep into the shadows on a shoulder of the road below. Too far away to see any hint of a driver. Odd time for someone to be visiting.

The wind had picked up, skimming the top of the canyon and whirling grit into his eyes. He dismounted, knowing Zephyr would wait in the nearby vicinity. He'd bought the quarter horse from a man who'd kept him half starved and left him to suffer the pains of two fractured ribs. It had taken Chad six months of patient coaxing to get the horse to even take an apple from his hand. Now Zephyr was his devoted companion and they both trusted one another completely. He was banking on the hope that Boss would not stray from Zephyr in this lonely spot.

"Stay close, Zeph," he said. "And keep an eye on Boss."

The horse blew air through his lips and began to nose the nearby clumps of grass.

Chad made his way to a spot from which he could observe the canyon. The failing light revealed a narrow path that carved its way through the jagged prongs of rock. He wasn't looking for anything in particular, but he couldn't shake the sense of unease. Something about the car…the time of day.

He heard a noise. Faint, low and unmistakable. Feet moving fast but stealthily. Who was sneaking around? His senses buzzed on high alert. He ducked low and crept around a stout pinnacle of rock, peering into the dusk. And that was when the bottom dropped out of his stomach.

He thought he must be hallucinating—imagining the woman who'd cut out a slab of his heart with her betrayal.

All he could do was gape.

Dory Winslow, white-blond hair tucked in a dark baseball cap, slim in black jeans and T-shirt, made her way gingerly to a clump of scrub. She was unaware of his presence.

Breathing hard through the wallop to his stomach, Chad tried to focus. What was she doing? Why was she back in Driftwood after all these years, hunkered down in this isolated canyon?

Heart slamming against his ribs, he watched as she eased a clump of grass away with her sneaker to reveal a rolled-up sleeping bag. He could not see anything else as she bent to examine what looked like a make-shift campsite.

Sweat broke out on his brow and he realized he was holding his breath. He forced out an exhalation, unable to take his eyes off the woman he'd hoped would become his wife.

Chad was a quiet person, silent as much as he was allowed to be, but now the word would not stay inside him. "Dory," he said, too quietly for her to hear. Remnants of the anger that had burned him internally for five long years boiled afresh.

He'd not spoken again, but she turned as if she sensed him there.

She scanned above her, fighting the setting sun, which made it difficult for her to make him out at first. Then her eyes riveted on him, widening, her mouth slackening in shock.

As he wondered what he should say, someone else detached from the rocky shadows.

"Watch out," he yelled.

His shout was lost in the blast of a gunshot.

TWO

Two shots. Three. The fourth came so close, Dory could hear the whine of the bullet punching through the air. She made herself as small a target as possible, tumbling behind a lip of rock. A shard scraped her wrist. Electricity ricocheted through her nerves both at the gunshot and the sight of the man she'd glimpsed staring down at her.

Chad. She was mistaken, she told herself. But the facts insisted otherwise. Eyes the color of dark chocolate under thick brows, full lips and the familiar battered cowboy hat. She wondered if it still showed the message she'd inked under the band after their junior prom. *You are my everything.*

It was wrong, she knew now. No one could be her everything but God. The lesson had been excruciating to learn.

The sight of Chad had turned her steel resolve to glass, weakening from the aftershock of seeing him.

What did you expect, Dory? Did you really think you could find out the truth about Blaze without running into Chad? He still lived in Driftwood, after all, a small ranching town where secrets were hard to keep. She'd intended to find proof that Blaze, the teen who'd supposedly drowned in the boat sinking, was very much alive. Once she made the ID, she'd hand the matter over to the police to delve deeper.

Never, ever, had she meant to clap eyes on Chad Jaggert again.

Shock turned to irritation, and anger licked at her throat. What was he doing here now? Right in the middle of her pursuit? How had everything gone so colossally wrong? Tempting as it was to try to sort out the messy bundle, there was a more urgent matter than Chad.

She darted a look around the edge of stone. The shooter was concealed now, probably tucked safely behind the massive split rock with the tree growing out of it. She scanned the area for options. Behind was a crevasse big enough for her to cut back through, but she was not sure if it dead-ended or led to a possible escape. Alternately, if she could distract the shooter for a moment, she'd be able to sprint the hundred feet to the cover of a rock pile. From there she'd have a better view. Some private eyes she'd met carried concealed weapons, but she'd never felt comfortable with that. Now she second-guessed her decision.

Would Chad have had the sense to hole up somewhere? She had a flashback to their dating days when they'd come upon a burning car in a ravine with the door wedged shut. Chad had not hesitated for one second as he'd gotten off his horse and smashed the driver's window with a rock before pulling out the screaming mom and two terrified kids. No, Chad would not back down from the situation, she thought with a sinking stomach.

The hair on the back of her neck rose as a figure blotted out the faint stream of moonlight. She whirled, still in a crouch, to find Chad Jaggert not three feet away. The scream died in her throat. In an effort to get control of her somersaulting senses, she feigned calm. "Go back the way you came."

His gaze bored into her, down to the deepest parts, the still depths that she kept locked away even from herself. He was silent for the longest moment before he half turned.

Dory almost sagged in relief. He was leaving, just like she'd asked. The sharp pain that lanced her heart puzzled her. Why, when he'd left her so long ago, should it hurt when he did so again? Especially when that was exactly what she wanted—for him to ride away along whatever trail had brought him here.

When he suddenly about-faced and reached for her, she almost jumped.

His fingers locked around her wrist.

She jerked tight, hoping he could not feel the pulse pounding through her veins. "What do you think you're doing?"

"Getting you out of here."

His voice, the deep baritone she hadn't heard in years, sounded as familiar as a favorite song. *Knock it off, Dory.* "You're not going to manhandle me."

He looked momentarily stricken, his gaze flicking to his hand as if he hadn't realized he was touching her. "I don't…"

"Let go—" she started to say just as another two shots drilled into the rock above her right shoulder, peppering them both with sharp bits. Stifling a scream, she crouched even lower and scurried after him through the crevasse. The rock walls pressed in on either side, narrowing in places until they had to scuttle sideways as they rushed on. Clouds drifted over the moon, which slowed their passage along the stony ground. She watched her feet to keep from stumbling.

He stopped once when he banged his head, but he clamped his lips tight and did not utter a sound. Silent, just like she remembered. Chad, her quiet cowboy. But when they were in love all those years ago and he'd laughed, really let loose in those infrequent moments, the joy lit up his soul and hers, too.

Don't go down that torn-up old road, she told herself. There was nothing in that direction but pain.

They emerged higher up and scooted along until they found a spot screened completely by scrub, but with a better vantage point. They lay on their stomachs, peering into the darkness, and she tried to ignore the fact that his shoulder pressed against hers. He wriggled as he pulled a cell from his back pocket.

"No signal here," she said.

"Figured I might still be able to send a text."

The night closed in around them. A cool breeze snaked down her back.

"Why's he shooting at you?" Chad asked.

"Maybe he's shooting at you."

His eyebrow arched. "You gonna make this difficult?"

She fired a look back at him. "You made this difficult, Chad. You intruded on this situation. I had it handled."

"Yeah? Got a gun on you somewhere?"

She didn't dare drop her head. "There are other ways to make an ID."

"An ID? What's all that talk?" He scowled. "Thought you were a paralegal in your dad's firm."

She caught the hostile inflection when he spoke about her father.

"I'm a private investigator now." She was gratified at his sharp intake of breath, the widening of his thickly lashed eyes, until his face split into a mischievous grin.

"Dear Old Dad must have loved that career choice."

She glared at him, but his smile remained.

"At least he can't blame that decision on me," Chad said.

Not trusting herself to speak, Dory eased up to a sitting position, still crouched behind the branches, and he did the same. Ignoring him, she plotted her next move.

"So who's the shooter? Some cheating husband you're tracking?"

"Chad, it really isn't your concern. Go back."

He let loose with a derisive snort. "And leave you here to get shot?"

"I'm not going to get shot."

"So sure of that? Why?"

"Because I'm good at what I do, and he's got a six-shot revolver. He stole the gun with only one magazine from a guy at a halfway house, and he's got zero money for more ammo."

Chad gaped. "How do you know all that?"

She couldn't help enjoying his surprise. "Like I said, I'm good at what I do." It took all her self-possession not to look at him, instead scanning the steep slope below for the fastest way to get from their hiding place to her fugitive's position.

He laid a palm on her arm, firmly but with gentleness. She almost closed her eyes against the agony that contact awakened. "You can't go down there. He could have another gun."

"I don't think so."

"You're going to possibly get shot on an 'I don't think so'?" He shook his head once, in the same decisive way she'd known him to do when they were dating. "No way."

She detached herself with a jerk. "Chad," she said, "you don't get to tell me what to do. I take care of myself."

"Yeah," he said. "That much I already know."

The comment stung. Five years ago, she'd given the police the truth, enough that they'd convicted Chad's father of boating under the influence and causing the death of Mary Robertson and her stepson, Blaze. She couldn't have done otherwise. Yes, she'd shared too much information with a man who'd later turned out to be a reporter, but she'd been naive. She bit back the mass of anger building inside as she considered Chad.

"This doesn't concern you." *Not until I have all the pieces put together.* "Go home."

In typical Chad fashion, he didn't reply right away. She almost believed she'd convinced him, but when she started her downward creep, keeping to the cover of the clumped grasses as best she could, Chad started right down behind her.

She suppressed a groan of pure despair.

Chad Jaggert could not become involved in this. She would never reveal what he'd walked away from all those years ago.

Her decision, her secret, their daughter.

Dory moved so fast that Chad had to scramble to keep up with her. He was surprised his addled brain could manage the task. All sorts of strange emotions bumbled around inside him like a runaway tumbleweed.

"Go back to your ranch. I don't want you here, okay?" Her voice was a whispered shout.

Though a dozen responses stampeded Chad's head as he crept along in her wake, they refused to assemble themselves into anything helpful. Words weren't his strong suit. Dory'd always been able to talk circles around him. Her honey-colored eyes when she glanced at him were unreadable, strange yet so familiar. The lush curve of her mouth drew into an angry line. When she stopped to get her bearings, he fired off the most obvious question.

"What are you planning to do?"

"My job," she snapped back. "Now go away."

"Who are you after?"

He could still pick up the slight arch of her delicate brow, the one that meant she was ready to tell him off in no uncertain terms. Instead she blew out a breath, staring into the canyon that was dissolving into darkness. When she turned back to him, she pulled off the black baseball cap, finger-combed her hair away from her cheeks and settled the cap on her head again.

It took him right back to summer days at the shore, piloting his father's twenty-five-foot fishing boat, *The Second Wind*, into the chill waters of Roughwater Harbor. That summer after they'd graduated high school, they would swim and then she'd lay on the deck to dry. Her hair was as luminous as the interior of an abalone shell. There hadn't been another place in the world he'd rather be than on that boat...until the accident that killed two of his father's clients.

He remembered arriving on the dock late, after a morning spent with Dory, looking out across the choppy waters of the harbor and seeing *The Second Wind* on its side. He recalled the terror he'd felt, leaping into the motorboat and flying across the water to find his father bobbing unconscious in a life vest. Friend and sometimes deckhand Tom Rourke swam in a panic with the limp body of Mary Robertson in his arms. Blaze, her stepson, was gone, swept out to sea.

Dory was about to plunge onward again when he tried once more. "Who are you after?"

"It's not the time to discuss it."

He stopped and she did, too. "You tell me right now, or I'm not leaving." He could not read her expression completely, but he knew her well enough to discern that she both believed the threat and resented his making it.

"Who are you after, Dory?" he repeated.

"This isn't your business. Why are you here, anyway?"

"My question first."

She folded her arms. "I'm working a case."

"Your private-eye job?"

"Not exactly."

"What's that mean?"

She shoved her hands into her pockets. "Can't you just leave it be?"

"Nope. So tell me or I stick to you like a barnacle on a boat."

She almost smiled. Almost. "A barnacle?"

He nodded solemnly. "On a boat."

All traces of humor vanished. "You're costing me time."

"So get to the truth, instead of trying to put me off."

She inhaled and blew out a breath. "You're not giving me any choice."

"Sure I am. Tell or I stay. That's a choice."

She rolled her eyes, a frown furrowing her forehead. He saw her come to some sort of a difficult decision. "It's going to be a shock," she said finally.

A tiny quiver of fear wriggled through his gut. Something big had brought her here. Something dangerous.

"I'm after Blaze Turner."

She'd spoken softly, but the name sounded in his ears like the boom of thunder. "What?" he managed to choke out.

"You heard me."

He'd heard, but he couldn't believe it.

Blaze, Mary Robertson's stepson? The man who'd fallen from his father's boat five years prior and was presumed drowned? Chad was suddenly back there again, hauling his father into the overloaded motorboat, as Tom did the same with Mary. Rocky had been unresponsive but breathing. Mary had been deathly still, water coursing from her limp hair over a face as pale as the white-topped waves.

I can't find Blaze, Tom Rourke had shouted as he'd tried desperately to perform CPR on Mary, hands shaking with each compression. Chad fought the wind-driven waves, desperate for any sign of the missing man. The weather had proved his enemy, an incoming storm heaving the water into foamy mountains that hammered the craft and dragged the boat debris in the direction of the open ocean.

His brain told him he'd somehow misunderstood her. But there was no mistaking Dory's seriously steely expression.

Blaze Turner was alive.

THREE

Chad was so shocked by her revelation that he stopped short. If things had been different between them, she might have reached out a hand to ground him. There was nothing, she knew, she could have said that would have unnerved him more. Except, perhaps, the one secret about them having a daughter that she would never tell him. Ever.

"Explain," he finally demanded, voice hoarse.

She started along the rocky trail then paused and turned back. "I can't go into it now. There's no time." But his look cut at her, the twin strands of pain and disbelief glowing in his chocolate irises.

Dory gave herself a moment to pare down her mountain of suspicion and data to the barest essentials. "Okay. I was at the police station in Sand Dune, filing a report for a client, when a couple of the cops brought in a guy they'd arrested for robbing someone at an ATM. There was a witness seen in the bank's video who may or may not have had something to do with planning the robbery. He was identified by a local as Brian Upton, but the cops couldn't locate him to get a statement."

"What does that have to do with—"

She held up a finger to stop him.

He winced but didn't interrupt this time.

"The local said Brian mentioned he was heading to the Driftwood area."

"Still doesn't prove—"

She laid a hand on his arm, fingers grazing his wrist. Her pulse buzzed at the contact and she hastily released her hold. "He described a detail about Brian that caught my attention."

Chad arched a dubious eyebrow.

"He has a tattoo of a spider on the back of his neck."

She saw his eyes widen.

"Lots of people might—"

She cut him off again. "A tarantula inked in blue with yellow eyes."

His mouth opened but he didn't speak.

"I wanted to be completely sure before I took it to the police."

It was as if Chad hadn't heard her. "So you're saying that all these years Blaze was pretending to be dead?" His dark gaze roamed the rocky ground until it riveted to hers. "Why?"

"I don't know yet, but I'm going to find out."

His eyebrow quirked with a second question that harpooned her soul. "Why would you care?"

And suddenly the years fell away and she was an almost-twenty-year-old, staring at the man whose love had turned to anger, his devotion to dismissal. It was the moment her heart disintegrated into tiny grains of sand. The day she'd started trying to figure out how to live without him.

She remembered their conversation, how his dark eyes had been pools of bottomless brown...

How could you tell the police my father's drinking was out of control? He's being accused of boating under the influence and manslaughter.

I told the truth, Chad. I didn't want to hurt him or you.

Yeah? I'm sure your daddy urged you to run right on down and spill everything you knew. You gave them plenty of backstory.

My dad works for the DA's office. He's an officer of the court. I couldn't...

He's a hateful meddler who never wanted me in your life and he's jumping for joy right now.

Things had only gotten worse from there. So much worse in ways he didn't even know about.

Dory forced down the leaden lump in her throat. "So now you know what I know. I'm going after him to get a positive ID. Alone."

"Not anymore."

She glared and shushed him. "Quiet. You're going to mess things up, and he'll flee."

Chad didn't answer, simply gave her his back as he peered through a screen of bushes into a tight ravine. "He's down there, heading for that offshoot canyon. It funnels into a pinch point that exits on the beach. Walls are too steep to climb. There's only one way out unless he doubles back to the opening. I'll make sure he doesn't do that."

"Chad." Her clipped tone carried on the night air as she strove for a calm she did not feel. "This is my case. You're not welcome here." *Or anywhere in my life.*

The glimmer of moonlight painted him in silver, his expression as hard cast as if he'd been fashioned from the metal itself. "It's not your case," he said quietly. "It never was." Then he moved to his left and started rapidly down the steep ground that would lead him to the mouth of the ravine.

Not your case. Chad saw it as a tragedy that had ruined his father with her help. What had she done, telling him the truth now? But he would have known if she'd tried to lie. They'd once been so bonded, he could tell what she was thinking without a word between them. She'd learned to decipher his barest flicker of expression that spoke volumes. Now he was silent, moving against the darkness.

She knew she'd awakened a fire inside him that would not be quenched until he got the truth. It was the same fire that burned inside her own soul.

You'll have to find out the facts together since he won't leave.

His father had only been released from jail six months before. She imagined it would be next to impossible for Rocky to find another job working on boats. The gossip about what he'd done was still alive and well in Driftwood, no doubt.

The scandal had started all those long years ago when she'd spoken to that reporter her father had insisted would help Rocky present his side of the story. The reporter had done nothing but produce a sensation-seeking story that had painted Rocky as a heartless drunk. Her father's manipulation of her had left scars that had only started to heal since she'd become a Christian. Thus far, she had not experienced any heart-mending whatsoever where Chad was concerned.

Her conscience pricked at her as she took over the lead down the trail. Maybe she did owe Chad at least a token involvement in the case.

Or maybe she was making the biggest mistake of her life.

* * *

Chad wished he were wearing better shoes, since his cowboy boots skidded on the gritty terrain. He didn't allow it to slow him down. Nothing would hinder him after Dory had dropped her bombshell.

Blaze Turner, the victim who had supposedly died due to his father's negligence, was alive and well, and Chad intended to find out why. Another question lurked just under the surface. Why did Dory care? Why was she risking herself to root out the truth? Didn't sound like she was being paid as a PI to find him. There were other options. Alert the police and let them handle it; even contact Chad anonymously if she didn't want to talk to him directly, which clearly she hadn't.

When he accidentally trod on her heel, she rounded on him. "Chad, you need to get out of here right now. I will handle this."

He turned and pressed a finger to his lips. "Quiet, remember?"

Even in the darkness, he imagined he could see her color rise, an angry flush backlighting the scatter of freckles across her nose. Dory was quite simply adorable, but he'd learned the hard way that there was plenty of strength under that sweet facade.

"You said if I told you, you would go."

"No, I said if you didn't tell me, I would stay. I've decided to stay anyway."

He ignored her sputtering, picking his way ahead of her as best he could. He had to lean back against the sharp downward pitch of the trail. Fortunately, the chaparral and sagebrush concealed their progress. Still, it was a relief when they reached the bottom, where the ground was slightly mucky.

Moisture collected along the periphery of the river, which surged in the darkness. They both paused to listen as the wind barreled across the riverbed, blasting them with cold.

Dory didn't seem to register the chill. "There," she said, pointing to a spot a couple hundred feet upriver.

It wasn't noise that gave away Blaze's location but a quick flash of light. The barest gleam perhaps caused by his checking his phone for messages.

Could be, Chad thought, it was an advantage that cell communications were disrupted by the canyon walls. He could not summon his brothers for help, or local cop Danny Patron, but neither could Blaze contact anybody.

"He's above us, at our eleven o'clock," Dory murmured into his ear. Her warm breath teased shivers up his spine. He nodded and crept forward. No use telling her to stay back. She wouldn't listen any more than he had. "Got to cut him off before he exits the canyon."

She stayed right behind him as they skirted the edge of the river, the rippling water covering their footfalls.

Rock scraped on rock from somewhere above them. A shower of debris rained down, plonking off Chad's hat and peppering their shoulders. The nearest cover was a bend in the canyon, a small hollow that allowed them to dive in and avoid most of the falling detritus.

Dory was breathing hard as her worried gaze met his. "Natural occurrence or does Blaze have help?"

Chad retrieved his hat. "Dunno. You're the one with all the information. He knows he's being followed. You tipped your hand."

"No, you did." She poked an accusing finger at his chest. "You stuck yourself in the middle of it all, and the noise gave me away."

Another rock plummeted so close it almost struck his shoulder. "Probably we should talk about this later."

The cascade slowed and gradually stopped. Chad sneaked a look. "No movement from above. Blaze is likely still beelining for the beach. I'm going to head him off at the pinch point."

"No, you're not," Dory said, scuttling out of their hiding place before he could unfold his six-foot frame. She raced past him, and by the time he'd gotten free, he'd lost her in the darkness.

"Dory," he whisper-shouted, but there was no answer save for the moaning wind. He didn't dare activate his phone light, so he waited until the clouds eased away from the moon long enough for him to pick out the sliver of riverbank. She'd obviously chosen a delicate path that both kept her out of the water and close to the sheltering rock walls.

Two minutes of dedicated pursuit and he caught a glimpse of her, hunched over, soldiering on through a narrowed throat of rock. A cascade of grit hit his cheek. He jerked a look up. Outlined against the sky at the top of the canyon was a precariously balanced boulder.

Was it a trick of the shadows or did he see a figure pressed close to the massive rock? He froze, catching the silhouette again, someone leaning against the granite. No, not leaning—pushing.

His shouted warning was buried in a groan as the boulder gave way and hurtled downward. The rock wall shuddered with the impact of the crashing stone. It smashed with such violence, the noise was like a bomb detonating. His ears pulsed. He almost lost his footing as a granite fragment clipped him on the knee. The sonorous boom nearly deafened him. Though he could not see where the boulder had come to rest through the roiling dust and grit, the noise died away as quickly as it had started.

Heart pounding, he ran to the spot he'd last seen her. There was a pile of rock where the opening had been only a moment before. His cry froze in his throat. The impact of the boulder had crushed the passageway.

"Dory," he shouted, but he could see no movement except for the billows of dust that stung his eyes, obliterating any signs of life.

FOUR

Vibrations rolled through her and it felt as though the sky itself had caved in. All around, the canyon walls rumbled and cracked, coughing forth stones that struck her shoulders as she caged her arms around her head. Rolling into as small a bundle as she could manage, she tucked herself tight under a lip of rock and prayed. The cacophony reached deafening levels. Her scream was muffled as dirt poured into her mouth before she clamped it shut.

There was no time to regret her hastiness in following Blaze into the canyon, not a moment to process what she would be leaving behind if the walls continued to unload on top of her. There was only thunder and shuddering shock waves and her own ink-black fear.

Her hiding place creaked and groaned as if it would give way at any moment. The tiny rock fort could not protect her much longer. She hoped it was not time for her to die. There was so much she had left to do, so many ways she had not yet grown into the person God wanted her to be. She could sense the presence of the massive burden ready to annihilate her from above.

The next moment, it was over. The earsplitting sound ebbed away into something much softer. Slow, sliding, trickling debris moved around her in a blanket of grit. But the walls stopped shaking and Dory could hear the beating of her heart, which proved to her senses, if not her brain, that she had lived through it.

I'm alive. Thank You, God. Tears squeezed through her tightly closed lids. Breathing hard, she forced her eyes open.

The darkness was profound. Terror clawed at her throat. Had she lost her sight? Was she buried in a coffin of rock? She blinked hard until tiny glimmers of light began to appear through the gloom, pinpricks of precious gold. She tried an exploratory stretch of her arms. Dust and debris slid and settled around her. As her vision adjusted, she realized she was still under the lip of rock. Above her, a massive boulder was wedged tightly across the top of the opening, blotting out the emerging stars. If it had not been for her small sliver of granite, she would undoubtedly have been crushed. A sharp stab of fear hit her again, deep in her belly.

Just breathe. That's all you have to do right now.

Swallowing hard, she tried to figure out next steps. The collapse blocked her from climbing upward. Rock and dirt swaddled her so tightly, she was afraid she might be buried alive if she tried to slither backward. There was no way to reach behind and get her phone out of her pocket. She had little hope that it would work anyway.

Chad, she thought suddenly. He was out there. He must have seen what happened. Unless he'd been caught in the avalanche, as well. Her stomach seized up. No. Chad was quick and strong and resourceful. He would get help. She pictured him running for his horse, galloping back to the ranch to raise the alarm. Suddenly she realized she was crying.

She'd come back to make amends, to set right the injustice visited on Chad's father. How had it all gone so very wrong? If Chad hadn't shown up, she'd be dead and buried, and no one would even know until someone found her car and put the pieces together.

"Stop feeling sorry for yourself," she hissed. If there was one thing she could not abide, it was self-pity. Though she couldn't free her hand to wipe her face, she turned her cheek to her shoulder and rubbed away the tears. *Better. Now find a way out.* If she was going to give Rocky his life back, she was going to have to save her own first.

She considered for a moment how her body was oriented underneath the lifesaving rock shelf. Her only chance was to move in what she figured was an easterly direction, away from the entombing pile toward the riverbed.

As she began to inch along, digging her shoes into the mess for traction, the earth moved with her, like a womb of soil. Rock shifted all around. Her pulse accelerated. Would she be able to free herself or would leaving her shelter mean she'd be crushed in a matter of moments?

One lesson she'd learned after her life had fallen apart five years before: there was nothing on the planet that could not be snatched away in a heartbeat.

All right, God. I know You decide if I live now or die, but I'm going to give it everything I've got.

With a quick squeeze of the locket around her neck for comfort, she began to slither into the unknown.

Chad danced over rolling rocks as he sprinted to the place beneath where the boulder had teetered precariously before settling. It looked as though the face of the canyon wall had sloughed off and collapsed. Every nerve in his body was taut as wire. Dory had to be visible, had to be standing somewhere safe against the treacherous mass, but he could catch no glimpse of her through the billows of airborne dirt.

"Dory!" he shouted. Only the pattering bits of rock answered him as they continued to fall. He pushed closer, climbing around larger fragments and plowing through others. He reached the edge of the collapse, shouting her name again and again.

He grabbed his phone and willed it to pick up a signal. Nothing. He considered running for Zephyr and galloping back to the Roughwater. There would be ranch hands there who could help and Uncle Gus. He turned to sprint, but something in him would not move, could not leave her there alone. Whether she was alive or dead, he was simply unable to run away even for a few moments.

"Come on, come on," he urged himself. "Think." He dropped to his knees, trying to assess where she'd been standing when the boulder broke loose. No, it hadn't broken loose. He felt certain it had been set in motion by Blaze. He had no time to consider that now. Rock shards bit through the denim of his jeans. He bent forward onto hands and knees, tracing a seam of cliff. Was there a protrusion there where she might have sought shelter?

He crawled closer, avoiding a fragment that fell and bounced to his left. The whole thing might just collapse at any moment if that giant boulder continued to shift. It was creaking like the old wood floor in the bunkhouse where he slept.

Slowly he started at the base of the pile, scooping palmfuls of dirt as he'd witnessed Liam's dog Jingles do countless times to burrow out of any kind of confinement. But unlike the exuberant dog, Chad worked carefully, easing each handful away, listening for further sounds of collapse. He continued until sweat soaked his shirt. He stopped to wipe his brow and turn on his cell phone flashlight.

Each moment increased his panic. What if…? Teeth gritted, he started afresh, digging until the pile started to tremble. He stopped, fearing he'd instigated another collapse. After a couple of seconds, he realized that the tiny movement was continuing, caused not by his actions or the teetering boulder.

He flopped on his belly. "Dory!" he shouted. Had he heard a reply or was it the slamming of his pulse? He started in again, shoveling the dirt away until his fingers were scraped raw.

There was no answer to his insistent shouting and his panic was about to be taken over by despair. Wind chilled his sweat-spangled brow as he sat back on his haunches and strained his ears to their limit.

Boots pounded over the ground.

Liam was suddenly at his side. "Was getting into my truck and I felt the ground shake. Saw dust rising from a collapse. Worried you might be close, so I called the cops and hightailed it here. Status?"

"Dory got caught as part of the cliff gave way. I think the guy who shot at us pushed the boulder over."

Liam jerked a look at him. "Dory? Your former girlfriend?"

He answered with a curt nod.

Liam took that in. "Got cops rolling. Will check for the squirter."

Chad had picked up enough military jargon from Liam to know "the squirter" was a person running away from a military attack. He didn't want to take the time to explain that this particular person was a guy who had been missing for five years and presumed dead. Liam didn't need to know that at the moment. He would recognize an enemy when he saw one.

Chad had moved a small hill of earth by the time Liam reappeared and resumed his spot on his stomach next to Chad.

"Nada. Can you hear any movement?" Liam asked.

Chad listened again. Nothing except the slow cascade of earth.

Liam put a hand on Chad's shoulder and he realized he'd not replied. He shook his head.

Another set of running feet announced Danny Patron. They rose to greet the police chief. He ran a hand through his thatch of red hair as he surveyed the collapse. "Fire department is on the way, but I'm not sure they're equipped to handle this. We got a victim in there?"

"Dory Winslow," Chad said.

Danny assumed the same shocked expression Liam had a moment before. "You mean the Dory Winslow who used to be your...?"

"Yeah," Chad said. "That one."

Danny closed his mouth. "Right, then. I've got a shovel in my trunk. I'll get it."

"Can you put out a BOLO for Blaze Turner?" Chad said.

Both Danny and Liam stopped and stared for the second time.

"Isn't that the name of the fella who drowned on your dad's watch?" Liam asked.

"Yeah. He's alive. Dory was tracking him. She's a PI."

Danny's face shifted in the moonlight from disbelief

to befuddlement. "And I thought I'd heard everything after fifteen years doing this job."

A trail of sliding dirt caught their attention.

Liam pressed his fingertips to the soil. "Hard to tell if it's the ground shifting or—"

Chad fell to his knees and laid his face on the dirt. He felt a tiny pulse against his cheek. "Dory!" he shouted.

Overhead, the boulder slid a few inches, raining more debris down on them.

He was about to shout her name again when something moved in the massive pile of earth. Heart in his throat, he watched as a hand thrust upward from the ground, white in the tarry night.

Instantly he fell onto his belly, grabbing at her fingers. They were cold in his grasp, trembling.

He started whisking away the dirt like a maddened gopher, Liam doing the same on his side.

In a matter of moments, they'd uncovered her arms and burrowed back to the spot where her head was sheltered by a rock structure. She blinked at them.

Chad was so relieved that she was alive, he almost whooped aloud. Grabbing her wrists, he began to pull her free when Danny shouted, "Stop!"

Immediately, he ceased.

Danny pointed a finger up toward the boulder.

The rock overhead moved, creaking and groaning.

They all went dead still, frozen, waiting for it to steady. Or…fall?

Chad squeezed Dory's wrists and she, too, stopped moving. Breath held, Chad waited as the boulder shimmied above them.

Would it hold? Or would it plummet?

FIVE

Dory felt the hands gripping her go still. "Pull me out," she wanted to shriek, but the pressure on her wrists increased to the point of pain. *Wait*, it seemed to say. So she counted the beats of her heart, stilling herself with an iron will she hadn't known she possessed.

Without warning, the squeezing grip changed to pulling and she was yanked through earth that undulated around her. One moment, she was trapped in a shroud of dirt, and the next, Chad had pulled her free.

The elation was so sweet she could taste it. Her senses dizzied for a moment and she wanted to stay there on all fours, feeling the air on her face, the fresh, cool wind that spoke of the sea and grasslands. Instead she was being picked up, flopped over Chad's shoulder.

"Let go," she said against his back, but her words were drowned in the horrible din. From her head-down position, she saw the boulder shimmy loose of its temporary cradle and smash downward, obliterating anything in its path. Loose rock, a crooked tree, the rock face—everything showered downhill until it finally hit the bottom. The impact annihilated the space she'd occupied only three minutes prior.

The boom struck at her eardrums. Her body flopped helplessly as Chad flat-out sprinted to avoid the flying debris. When he finally slowed, he rolled her off his shoulder and set her on the nearest flat rock. Her vision whirled as she perched there, panting. The earth and her senses steadied in slow unison. Finally, the ground was still and she could discern up from down.

She saw a taller man with Chad. He had chiseled features and coppery hair. She guessed he was part of the clan she'd heard about that'd taken Chad under its wing when Rocky's drinking got out of control. She'd met Gus and Ginny Knightly and Mitch Whitehorse, but not the others. Danny Patron was there, too, talking into his radio. She'd spoken to him in depth after the drowning, though it had been the Coast Guard that had actually arrested Rocky.

All three of them were staring at her.

"Ma'am," said the taller man, his voice colored by a Southern drawl. "Name's Liam Pike. I'm Chad's brother, more or less. I was deployed for most of your… I mean, while you and Chad were…" He cleared his throat. "How are you feeling, if I may ask?"

She coughed and wiped dirt from her eyes. "Shaken up, but okay." Another cough. "I think that lip of rock saved my life."

He nodded, smiling. "Excellent. Would you mind if I checked you over real quick-like? I was a Green Beret medic back in the day."

She allowed him to skim his fingers over her arms and legs for injury. He looked closely at her pupils and took her pulse.

"The ambulance is almost here, Miss Winslow,"

Danny said, "but Liam's the second-best thing in the meantime."

"I'm never second-best at anything," Liam shot over his shoulder, giving Dory a wink.

Chad did not take his eyes off her. "Could she be bleeding internally? Concussed?"

Liam straightened. "Hospital will make that determination."

"I'm okay," she said.

Chad started to speak again when a siren wail echoed off the canyon walls.

Liam glanced at Chad. "Siren?"

Chad nodded. She realized that Liam had some sort of hearing loss. A moment later, Liam acknowledged with a nod of his own as the sound became loud enough for him to detect. "That'd be the rest of the cavalry."

"How did you know to come here?" Dory said.

Liam grinned. "Aww, it's my job to keep my eye on little brother." The strobing lights of the ambulance bathed them all in eerie colors that cut through the dusk.

"She needs to talk to you," Chad said to Danny. "To fill you in on the guy she was tracking."

"No, I don't," Dory said. "I'm not done with my investigation yet."

Chad fisted his hands on his hips. "You most certainly are done. You nearly got killed."

"Because you interfered."

"You call saving you interfering?"

"Yes. I would have ID'd him already if you hadn't butted in."

He glared at her and she glared right back.

Liam and Danny exchanged amused glances.

Liam's mouth twisted in a grin. "Do y'all need half a minute?"

"No," they both said at once.

"Uh-huh," Liam said. "How's about I just scoot along, call my wife, and track down Zephyr and Boss while you two sort out what you want to do next."

"I'll just scoot right along with you," Danny said, "and get my officers sorted out. Back in a jiffy."

Dory caught Liam's low chuckle as he strolled away.

When they had a small cushion of privacy, she squared her shoulders. "This is my case."

"This isn't about you, Dory. This is about my dad and what happened to him."

"If the cops show too strong a presence, Blaze will bolt and you'll never find out the truth."

"Danny's a good man and a smart cop. He'll know what to do."

"It's not your call to make."

He thrust his chin out in that way. "Yes, it is. It was my family that got destroyed back then, Dory."

Your family. Oh, how little he knew. She swallowed hard, biting back the avalanche of feelings as the medics hustled over.

Chad was full of so many emotions, he figured the best course of action was to stay quiet and watch Dory until she reconsidered and could be handed over to the hospital people. Hopefully, they would know what to do with her, because he hadn't the vaguest notion.

He crossed his arms in front of his chest and tried to look elsewhere—at the canyon, at the settling dust, toward the ever-darkening sky—but could not keep from flat-out staring. If he hadn't known who he was looking at, he wouldn't have guessed his petite former girl-friend was perched in front of him. Her blond hair was completely brown with dirt, face streaked with grit. Her clothes were torn and caked with debris. Only the amber eyes were recognizable, but he thought there was something different about those, too.

The shock, no doubt.

He was reeling with it himself.

Waving off the paramedic who wanted to give him the once-over, he stood there feeling all kinds of awkward until Liam returned with Zephyr and Boss. Boss looked more relaxed. At least that had gone according to plan.

Danny approached Dory as the medic checked her blood pressure.

"I am going to be here awhile to secure the area. I'll track you down to hear all the details of how you got to be at the bottom of that big pile of dirt," he said with his customary smile. "Where can I find you?" He raised a hopeful brow. "The hospital?"

She shook her head. "I'll get a room in town."

"But you're…" Chad hedged.

She went still. "I'm what?"

"Well, I mean…" Chad looked at his boots.

Liam chuckled. "I think Chad is trying to tactfully point out that you look like you just crawled out of the bottom of a coal bin. Folks might be…er, hesitant to rent you a room. How 'bout you come bunk at the ranch tonight? Saddlery's got a cot and shower. Coffeepot even. My wife bunked there for a while before we were married."

"Absolutely not. I'll drive to town and…uh…" She

surveyed her ruined clothing with a sigh. "I guess I wouldn't rent me a room, either. I'll sleep in my car."

Chad jammed his hands on his hips. "Come on, Dory. One night at the saddlery and a shower, and you're gone in the morning. Why is that so hard to accept?" He knew the answer. *Because you're the one offering it.* He figured he was the one who should be upset about the arrangement. She'd betrayed him and his father and there was no changing that, even if she had nearly gotten herself killed.

He watched her struggling to find a better answer.

Liam didn't wait. "All right, then. It's settled." He handed a set of keys to Chad. "I'll take the horses back and call Aunt Ginny. You can drive Dory in my truck. We'll get someone to drive her car to the ranch. Meet you back there."

Chad felt a surge of relief for his bullheaded brother who always knew when not to take no for an answer, but his stomach knotted at the notion of being alone with Dory.

Danny nodded. "When I get clear, I'll come by the ranch to talk to you both."

After Danny departed, Chad set his jaw and waited for the medics to finish before he led the way to Liam's truck.

She was silent.

He was, too.

The short drive seemed endless. Each mile took him further back into the past to their last conversation.

I had to tell the truth. I'd seen him drinking the week before.

But not that day. You volunteered that. You sold out my father to please your own.

Her tears. His tortured breathing.

We can get past this, Chad.

And his answer.

No, we can't. We're done, Dory. I don't ever want to see you again.

He'd left with the engagement ring in his pocket and his heart turned to stone.

Five years later, that lump of stone was still where his heart should be.

He checked his watch. Almost ten. He hadn't called in at his father's trailer to check on him. Though he wouldn't admit it, he had scoured the dingy place while his dad had been out walking the beach the day before. He'd found no bottles. How would it affect his dad hearing that Blaze was alive?

Until Chad knew more, he'd do his best to keep the information to himself.

He pulled the truck onto Roughwater Ranch property and Aunt Ginny opened the saddlery door to meet them. She smiled at Dory, her silver pixie cut catching the light of the small lamp.

"Hello, Mrs. Knightly," Dory said.

"I'm Ginny. Everyone calls me Aunt Ginny whether we're related or not. Good to see you again."

Dory offered her hand then seemed to notice the grime coating her skin. Aunt Ginny seized her palm anyway and shook her hand.

"I'm sorry to disturb you," Dory said. "I would have been fine sleeping in my car."

"My better half, Gus, is snoring fit to beat the band, so I was up anyway. I wouldn't have anyone sleeping in a car when there's a perfectly fine empty bed here." She handed Dory a folded towel. "I put clean sheets on the bed and the coffeepot is set for six tomorrow morning. Breakfast is at seven in the main house after the men are back from morning chores."

"But…" Dory said.

Aunt Ginny waved her off. "Better tell her about Meatball," she said to Chad as she passed through the door.

Dory stood there with her mouth open for a few seconds. "Meatball?"

Chad was about to answer when Liam strolled through the open door, a wriggling bundle under his arm.

"Ma'am," he said. "Sorry, I forgot to mention you'd have a bunkmate. I got my hands full with Jingles, the biggest mess of a ranch dog you've ever clapped eyes on. I can't handle two mutts." He thrust the animal into Chad's arms. "Night, then."

"Hey—" Chad started, but his brother was already gone. He sighed as Meatball yipped.

"So that's Meatball?" Dory said with a slight quirk of a smile.

"Yeah. Jingles nosed him out onto the property. We figure he's some kind of cross between an Australian shepherd and a hound." Chad shifted the wiry blond dog and scratched behind his triangle ears. Meatball rewarded him with exuberant licks under his chin. "Someone dumped him, we figure, since he's a tripod. Just a puppy still." He showed Dory the place where Meatball's back leg should be. "Gets along fine on three. Wants to be a ranch dog so bad, but he was emaciated when Jingles found him and vet says he should be sleeping indoors at night till he's stronger."

The silence set in as he tried to think about what to say next. There didn't seem to be much more to discuss about the puppy. Should he grill her further about Blaze? Surely not while she was standing there filthy and tired. He still had some sense of decency, didn't he?

When would Danny arrive to get their statements? What should he do in the meantime? Linger? Go sit in the truck? Go back to the bunkhouse?

"Come on," she said, stretching out her arms.

He went hot and prickly at first, thinking she meant to hug him, until he realized she was waiting for him to hand her the dog. Meatball immediately nestled in her arms and began his tongue swab of her chin. She laughed. Her hearty chuckle zinged right to Chad's core. He'd never laughed so hard with anyone but Dory. Probably never would again.

Throat dry, he swallowed. They'd met over a dog, really. In high school, she'd been sent to detention for being late five days in a row. She'd been trying to track down a stray she'd seen sniffing around an empty lot as she'd walked to school. He'd been in detention for skipping school altogether to help his father on the boat.

School had never been his thing since he'd learned his mother had been having an affair with his freshman track coach. Though his mother had left and he and his father had moved to Driftwood in his junior year, the humiliation had clung to him. The new school hadn't been much better, except no one knew him and he'd met Dory, the girl who had changed everything. He'd loved her right through his last two years of high school and the almost three years after their graduation, until everything went up in smoke.

Meatball continued with the dog kisses.

"I'm going to take a shower," she said. "If my cell still works, I'll text you when Danny gets here."

Practical, always. They checked and found her phone operational. She didn't ask for his number, so he figured she still had it. Hers was still in his phone, too. For some reason, he hadn't gotten around in five years to deleting it.

"Come on, Meatball," she said, putting the puppy in the box on the floor they'd set up for his bed.

The dog set into an immediate fuss, whining and turning agitated circles. She relented, bending to swoop him up again, a silver locket spilling free from her shirt.

Whose picture was in it? he wondered. A new man? Stomach churning, he discarded the thought.

"Okay, Meatball, I guess you can sit on a towel while I shower, but no whining," Dory said, kissing the dog between the ears. She glanced at Chad—a quick look then away. "I'll…see you later."

The notion sent his nerves tumbling. See her again and do what? Talk to the woman who'd made him believe in himself just before she'd destroyed him? Thinking about it cinched knots into his gut. How had she turned up and upended his life in the space of a few hours?

He wanted to get on Zephyr and lose himself in the endless green pastures.

But if cooperating with Dory was what he had to do to clear his father's name, then he'd somehow bear it.

With a silent nod, he strode out of the saddlery.

SIX

Dory was delighted to be clean. It had required all the hot water the shower could provide, but she was gloriously free of grit, from her hair to her toes. Meatball had taken his guard duties seriously, standing at attention inside the bathroom door the whole time. Then he'd assisted in drying off her ankles with his tongue until she'd pulled on the clean clothes Aunt Ginny had left for her.

Out the small front window, she noticed someone had delivered her car and parked it under the trees alongside the wide front road.

The dog waggled his hind end when she looked at him.

"Meatball, I know someone who would love to meet you." She sat in a beat-up leather chair and snuggled the dog. Her nearly five-year-old daughter Ivy's bright eyes would light up at the sight of this happy puppy. Her throat thickened. Ivy would be tucked into bed now at Grandma and Grandpa's house, a stuffed animal under each arm.

It was time to get a pet, she decided. It would have to be a small one, since they rented a tiny one-bedroom house they could barely afford and there was an upcoming move to Arizona in the offing. Her father would not agree, at first, but he would relent.

She was hit by a sudden pang of doubt. Was she doing what was best for Ivy, chasing down Blaze Turner?

Since she'd become a Christian, she'd been convicted in her soul that she should help Rocky Jaggert. If it was within her power, she wanted to undo the part she'd played in his arrest before she moved to Arizona. That was the person she wanted to show her daughter, a woman who tried to live a godly life, who took responsibility for her actions. She wanted Ivy to be proud of her mother.

But who would show the little girl what a father should look like?

We're done, Dory. I don't ever want to see you again.

She could have told Chad about Ivy. Lately her prayers had led her to the possibility that he had a right to know about his own child. But worse than losing Chad would be having him stick around out of guilt and duty. That she could not abide.

Swallowing a sudden lump in her throat, she laid Meatball in his box. "I need some rest," she told him. "Things will be clearer when I'm not so tired."

Body aching from dozens of scrapes, she climbed under the clean sheets, reveling in their softness. She laid the locket on the side table along with her phone, which was set to loud so she would not miss Danny Patron's call.

Meatball began to whine from his box.

"It's okay. I'm right here." Her eyes grew heavy. Blaze popped into her mind. She knew it had been him in that canyon. For five long years, the world had thought him dead. What was he doing in Driftwood now? And why had he tried to kill her? The panic she'd felt at being trapped and nearly smothered ballooned in her chest until a soft bundle launched itself next to her. Meatball immediately burrowed under the sheet, squirming up to Dory's side.

I belong up here next to you, she was sure he was saying. *See? Now everything's as it should be.*

Everything was absolutely not as it should be, but she thanked God for her blessings, including the odd creature snuggled up next to her.

An hour later, the buzzing of her phone awakened her. It was a text from Danny sent to both her and Chad.

Apologies. Held up at the collapse. Okay to get your statements tomorrow morning at ranch?

Chad's answer was immediate. He had obviously not been sleeping.

Yes. We'll be here.

She felt a flash of irritation that he would answer for her. "*We'll* be here." It reaffirmed her decision not to tell him about Ivy.

There's no "we" anymore, Chad. Just like you wanted it.

The smartest plan of action was clear. Talk to Danny. Help with the investigation as best she could. Get out as quickly as possible.

Mind settled, she closed her eyes until a sound caught her.

Glass breaking.

She sat up so abruptly her head spun. Meatball popped

his head from underneath the sheet and squirmed out as she bolted from the bed. Blaze was back to kill her. Terror coursed through her nerves.

Easy, Dory. The sound had been distant, not near the saddlery.

Heart thumping, she padded to the window, almost tripping on the dog.

It was just before 6:00 a.m., still dark as she peered out onto the long drive. Her car. She pressed closer. Yes, there was a shadow, splayed by the moonlight, near the front fender.

A human shadow.

Blaze?

As much as she dreaded the thought, there was only one course of action.

Fingers cold, she sent Chad a text.

Someone is breaking into my car.

As he read the text, Chad immediately yelled across the field to Mitch, pulled Zephyr into a tight circle and urged him into a gallop. They flew across the wet grass, stopping only to unlock a gate. Four minutes of hard riding and he was at the saddlery, sliding off the horse and grabbing his rifle.

His boots crunched over broken glass as he approached Dory's car. The front driver's-side window was busted, the hammer still lying on the front seat where it had been tossed. He checked the interior and started in on the clustered oaks by the time Mitch brought his mare, Rosie, to a halt.

"Gone," Chad reported. "Probably on foot."

Mitch readied his rifle. "I'll check the woods. Liam's

taking the ATV to sweep along the road. Stay inside with her until we call it clear."

Chad tied Zephyr to a post outside the saddlery to keep him from stepping on any broken glass. Dory opened the door as he jogged up. Her eyes were wide with fear. The look cut at him. He desperately wanted to say something to make that expression go away.

"No one there," he told her.

She stepped aside for him to enter. Meatball galumphed around, greeting Chad and hustling back to Dory.

"Did you see who it was?"

She shook her head. "No, but I have a good idea. Blaze."

"Why would Blaze do it? Why not run? He's got to know he'll be in trouble after what happened at the canyon."

"For whatever reason, he has business in Driftwood." He saw the muscles of her throat constrict. "And he's got business with me."

Chad strode to the window, more to hide his emotions rather than check for any sign of Mitch's return. "Well, I've got business with him, too. He owes me and my father an explanation." His phone buzzed with a call from Danny, so he filled him in.

Officers arrived within fifteen minutes to process the evidence at the car, and another quarter of an hour passed while they waited for word.

Mitch eventually let himself in. "Hello, Dory. I found nothing. Liam couldn't track him, either. We're all clear."

Chad shoved a hand through his hair and looked at

Dory. "What did he want in your car? Did you leave anything inside?"

She shook her head. "Only a jacket and some Cracker Jacks."

He almost smiled at that one. Since he'd first known her, Dory was passionately devoted to Cracker Jacks. Her collection of tiny prizes was a thing to behold. No one had been as grieved as Dory when the company discontinued the plastic trinkets. He'd not thought of that for a long time.

"Appears he was after information," Mitch said.

Chad saw Dory go pale.

"Car registration?" Chad guessed.

Mitch nodded. "It's gone. Did you have your vehicle registered to a business address or home?"

It took her a beat to get it out. "My business address in Rock Ridge." She blew out a breath. "At least he doesn't know where I live."

"All right." Mitch checked his phone. "Liam's at the house now and Danny just arrived. Family's gathered. Let's go over and brief everybody." Mitch made his way outside and strode off.

"I'll walk you over to the main house before I tend to Zephyr."

"You don't need to do that. I'm perfectly capable of…"

"Blaze could be on the property still."

"He's most likely gone, just like your brother said."

"I'm not willing to risk your safety on a 'most likely' even if you are a tough private eye." His tone was un-called for, and he knew it.

Her eyes narrowed. "Chad…"

"All right. Compromise. I'll ride Zephyr halfway

and keep eyes on you until you get to the main house before I go brush him down. Fair?"

"Fair. What about Meatball?"

"He can follow along. Jingles will be at the house if Liam's there. Aunt Ginny usually has a slice of bacon for each of them."

Dory walked to the side table and picked up her locket. It slipped through her fingers and fell, skittering toward his boots. The heart opened and he caught a quick glimpse of a smiling toddler. She snatched it up before he could get a proper look at the photo.

"Who's that?"

She didn't meet his gaze. Looking over his shoulder, Dory bobbed her chin. "We shouldn't keep everyone waiting." She hurried out, Meatball dogging her steps.

He untied Zephyr and climbed in the saddle.

Had he been nosy asking about the picture in the locket? Probably. But something in the way she grabbed at it stuck with him.

Five years, he reminded himself.

It had been five years since their relationship exploded. She could have met someone. Been married even. Had a family he knew nothing about. Why did that thought feel like swallowing a shard of glass?

You told her flat out you'd never forgive her.

You had good reasons.

God obviously hadn't meant for them to be together. So whoever was in the locket was her business.

Not quite settled in his spirit, Chad returned Zephyr to the barn and rubbed him down. Though he chafed to get to the main house to find out if there were any answers to the mountain of questions racing through his mind, Zephyr's care came first.

Once the quarter horse was fed and watered, Chad let him loose. Zephyr made his way over to Boss. The two horses exchanged a nickered greeting. Progress, he thought.

As expected, Meatball and Jingles were polishing off their slices of bacon on the Spanish-tiled entry floor. They seized the opportunity when he opened the front door to zip past him and bolt outside. He expected to find the family gathered in the great room. Instead he found Mitch and Jane and Liam's wife, Maggie, counting small, folded baseball jerseys. Charlie was playing on the floor with a collection of trains.

Mitch didn't exactly smile, but he seemed lit up from the inside. "Baseball uniforms," he said. "Jane's the team mom."

His wife laughed and flipped her dark braid over her shoulder. "Well, since I'm a florist, you're fortunate I didn't order them with poppies and roses all over."

Mitch did smile then. "We're the Tigers, so these are probably better."

Maggie held a jersey up for Chad to see. "Charlie's number one."

"Of course," Liam said, entering from the kitchen with a muffin in his hand. He nuzzled his wife's neck until she squealed. "What else would my nephew be?"

Jane pulled a face. "No bragging now, Coach Liam."

"I'm only the backup coach to Mitch and chief messenger boy. Aunt Ginny said to move you all into the kitchen."

"No can do," Maggie said, ducking Liam as he came in for another kiss. "I'm on my way to my shift at the Lodge. Scrambled eggs won't wait, you know."

Liam wrapped an arm around her shoulders. "I'll walk you to your truck."

"So you can steal more kisses?"

"Nah." Liam was serious now. "I told you about this Blaze character. Don't want our ladies wandering around alone till we corner this guy." He allowed a smile then. "But a few extra kisses won't hurt, either."

Chad followed Mitch and Jane into the kitchen and Liam joined them a moment later.

Danny, Aunt Ginny, Uncle Gus and Dory were already seated at the round table. In the middle was a haphazard spray of wilted wildflowers he'd seen Charlie present with great ceremony to Aunt Ginny. They all had plates of scrambled eggs and bacon in front of them. Aunt Ginny passed around a pot of coffee and a tray full of muffins.

Chad stalled for a moment by going to the cupboard to grab himself a mug. He could not stop the thought of Dory with another family. A man who might have given her all the things he'd dreamed about having— What was the matter with him? Being close to her again made his nerves skitter like a spooked colt. *Man up, Chad.*

As he headed for a chair, Liam scooted around him and sat next to Danny, leaving the only empty seat smack-dab next to Dory.

Inwardly, he groaned. Something about Liam's mischievous smile made him think his brother was enjoying the whole situation a bit too much.

Danny sipped coffee and sighed. "If only I could get this kind of coffee at the station. Sometimes Jenn and the kiddos come to deliver me a cup to save me from the swill."

Aunt Ginny filled Chad's cup. "How is your sweet little girl, Danny?"

"Doing great. You'd never guess she had a partial liver transplant two months ago. The hard part now is to keep her from running around too much. I thank the Lord every moment of every day for restoring our baby's life, and that's no exaggeration."

"Amen to that," Ginny said.

He drained his cup and Ginny refilled it. "Okay. Down to business, Dory. I've got someone going over your car to check for prints. For now, tell me from the beginning who you're tracking and why."

Dory recounted the story that led her to the man she believed was Mary Robertson's stepson, Blaze.

"Any theories about why he would disappear and then come back here?" Danny asked.

"It's nearly the anniversary of the boating accident," Dory said. "Next month will be five years."

The anniversary. Why hadn't he realized that?

Chad saw something kindle in Danny's expression.

"After five years, a missing person can be declared legally dead." Danny tapped his mug with a forefinger. "So could be he's rolled into town to claim his inheritance before that happens."

"Who gets the money if he doesn't?" Chad asked.

"I looked that up this morning. His aunt. Angela Robertson, Mary's older sister, is the next in line. I've got a call in to meet with her."

Liam took a hearty bite of muffin. "It's a big haul, that inheritance."

Uncle Gus wrapped an arm around Ginny's shoulders. "True enough. Mary's husband, Scott Turner, was the founder and CEO of a high-end motorcycle company. They had that gorgeous property along the cliff side. Doesn't seem like they were hurting for money, that's for sure."

Ginny frowned at him. "Gossip, Gus?"

"Just the truth, honey bun." He kissed her cheek. "Scott had the good sense to go into something besides ranching." His grin faded as he looked back at Danny. "But what did Blaze gain from playing possum all this time? He was nineteen at the time of the accident. Why hide?"

Chad's teeth ground together. "And let my dad take the rap for his death." A thought sizzled through his mind. "If this is Blaze, he might be able to shed some light on what really happened that day." He sensed Danny's hesitation, the awkward silence around the table. His frustration spilled out in a gush of words. "I know you all think it's cut-and-dried, that Dad was drinking and he capsized the boat, but maybe there's something more."

He felt Dory's gaze on him. "You must believe there's something else to the story if you came back here to track him."

"I'm not sure, Chad. I just know Blaze faked his death. That was enough for me to want to track him down. Your father shouldn't have been prosecuted for two deaths."

"You didn't defend Dad then. Why bother getting involved now?" The words, flung like acid, made her flinch.

Cheeks flushed, she turned to Ginny. "Thank you very much for your hospitality. It was more than kind of you. I'll be going now."

"You're leaving?" Chad said.

Still she didn't look at him. "Danny, you have my contact info. I'm going to pack up and I'll be out of here as soon as your officers release my car."

She got up and carried her plate to the kitchen sink, washing and wiping it dry. At once, everyone seemed to be extremely busy. Liam and Mitch kissed Ginny and left, Gus right behind them. Danny thanked Ginny again for the coffee and exited, also.

Ginny followed Danny. "I have some coloring books for your girls. I'll get them for you."

And then Chad was left alone with Dory and a deep well of uncertainty. Of one thing he was sure: he had been rude. Such a thing was inexcusable in Aunt Ginny's kitchen.

Letting out a breath, he tried again.

"I apologize for mouthing off. I know..." He cleared his throat. "I mean, I know you loved my dad, too."

"Love," she shot back. "I love your dad. I didn't stop loving him because you pushed me out of your life."

He studied his boots. "Anyway, I'm sorry. I'll clean the glass out of your front seat."

"No, thank you. I'll do it myself."

Her phone beeped and she checked the screen.

The change was instantaneous. All color drained from her face. Her mouth pinched in fear and she clutched the phone so hard her knuckles went white.

"I...I have to go."

"What's wrong?"

"Nothing. I have to go now."

He reached for her arm but she pulled away. "Never mind about the glass. It will be fine."

"I'll go with you. It will just take a minute."

"No." She snapped the word out like a cracking whip. "I have to be alone right now."

In a moment, she'd practically run, leaving the kitchen door open behind her.

What had spooked Dory? What message could have unsettled her to such a degree?

He made his decision in the span of ten seconds. She'd come here, upended his life, and she figured she'd disappear just as abruptly?

"Not gonna happen, Dory."

SEVEN

Dory shivered as she hurriedly grabbed her meager belongings from the saddlery. The text was burned into her mind.

Meet me at the old bridge at sundown. Don't bring the police.

The attached photo had flipped her heart into useless quivering.

Two faces pressed close together. Hers…and Ivy's. She'd forgotten about the personalized photo iPad cover she'd bought, the one she kept in the glove box. There were also some business cards with her cell phone number. She'd made it so easy for him.

Some private investigator.

The text had to be from Blaze. He didn't know where Ivy was, she told herself, her pulse beating against her throat. But now he knew her work address. She'd done enough online sleuthing to know that, with enough perseverance, most information could eventually be unearthed. Though she would be moving in a matter of months, her office was currently a scant twelve miles from the tiny home she rented for her and Ivy in Rock Ridge. It was fifteen miles distant from her parents' house, where Ivy was staying over spring break from the school where she was in a prekindergarten class.

"Calm down," she told herself. First, she dialed her parents' number. Her mother picked up.

"Hi, Mom. How are you and Ivy?" Her heart pounded until she heard the report.

"Great. We finished baking a chocolate cake with about three pounds of sprinkles on top. I don't know how we are going to even lift it from the counter to the kitchen table. She's in the bathroom, washing up. Are you okay? You sound worried."

"I'm fine. Thank you for watching her for a few days. Mom, um, I know this is going to sound weird, but can you keep her home until I get back? I mean, no park or playdates?"

The pause lingered. "Dory, what aren't you telling me?"

"It's the case I'm working on. Someone I'm tracking got my business address. I'm sure it's nothing, but I'd just feel better knowing Ivy was staying close to you."

"All right. Why don't you come home and work this thing out with your father? He'll know how to handle it."

Her father would go ballistic knowing she was in Driftwood trying to help Rocky. Worse yet, that she was working a case with Chad. His anger at Rocky Jaggert had a long history, stretching way back to his college days when both men wanted to date her mother, Sarah. Their bitterness had only worsened after her parents married.

Even after decades had passed, the tension flared

again when Rocky's wife had cheated on him with Chad's track coach. She'd abandoned the family, forcing them to move. Sarah had greeted single-father Rocky warmly when they'd moved to town, unperturbed when Chad and Dory started dating.

They're two nice kids. Why shouldn't they date?

Her father had been furious. *I don't want that boy anywhere near Dory.*

What he hadn't said shouted just as loudly. *And I don't want my wife anywhere near Rocky Jaggert.*

Why could her father not see that his wife was simply a woman with a warm heart and a soul brimming with compassion? She had no desire to resurrect a relationship with Rocky, but nothing would soften her father on the topic.

The kid is going nowhere. You can do better.

And later…the terrible weight of his anger when she'd revealed her pregnancy to her parents.

You're barely twenty years old. No degree, no husband, no job. Chad ruined your life, and you let him. How could you be so stupid?

The rupture to her heart had been insurmountable and she'd run away, enduring horrors she still did not like to recall. But after years of gradual healing, her father had grown to adore Ivy and his anger had cooled. She knew it was still there, though, lingering under the surface like flammable vapors waiting for a spark.

"Honey?" Her mother tried again. "Come home and talk it over with your father."

"I will, as soon as I finish up a few things. Please don't worry him, okay? Everything's under control." They chatted for a few minutes more before Dory ended the call.

It would not be long, she feared, before her father got wind of their conversation and began calling her himself. If she so much as breathed a word about Blaze, he would use all his contacts at the district attorney's office to aid in the search.

Blaze's warning blared in her mind. *Don't talk to the police.*

Maybe she should go to Danny anyway. But if Blaze thought she was trying to trap him, what would he do? She had no idea what kind of a man he was, aside from the investigation into his possible involvement in the ATM robbery, nor had she an inkling about why he'd come back. The smart thing would be to hand over the info to the police and get back to her daughter. But what if Blaze intended to hunt for Ivy?

She gritted her teeth. She remembered those long, hard days living in a cramped trailer in the middle of nowhere, the place she'd run to after the hateful scene with her father. Pregnant and scared, she'd worked three jobs to save up money so she and Ivy could live on their own. No handouts from her parents. No charity. She would take care of that little life. God allowed her to do that. She wouldn't let anyone get near her daughter without her permission.

Not Blaze. Or Chad.

Jaw tight, she dialed the texter's number.

The phone rang three times before someone picked up.

"Blaze?" she said. "Is that you?"

The voice was quieter than she'd expected, rough-edged, as if the speaker was a smoker. "Meet me like I told you."

"I'm not going to meet you. Tell me why you came back to Driftwood."

"Meet me," he snarled, "or you'll never know what happened."

"Why have you been playing dead all these years?"

"You know what to do." He paused. "That's a real pretty girl in the photo I texted you."

Rage hummed in her ears. "If you touch my daughter—"

The dial tone chirped in her ear at the same moment she realized she was not alone. Dread coiled in her stomach as she slowly turned around to find Chad standing in the doorway, staring at her. His wide-eyed shock told her he'd heard it all. Her secret was out now.

My daughter...

Slowly she pocketed the phone and braced herself to face what would come next.

The word bumped around his brain...*daughter.*

"You have a daughter?" he finally managed to ask.

Dory closed her mouth and wrapped her arms around herself. "It's not your concern."

"I...I didn't mean to pry. Sure, your business. Right." He hooked his thumbs through his belt loops. "You were talking to Blaze. He texted you, didn't he?"

A furrow appeared between her brows. He thought she wouldn't answer for a moment.

"My cell phone number was on a business card in my vehicle. Also, there was a picture of my daughter. He's trying to threaten me into meeting him."

Chad reached for his phone. "I'll call Danny..."

She held up a palm to stop him. "He said if the police are involved, we'll never know what happened."

"Danny will be discreet. He'll…"

She shook her head. "No. I'm going to meet him, Chad. I want to see for myself what kind of person he is. If I feel unsafe, I won't get out of the car."

He tried not to outright gape. "That's not gonna happen, Dory. Absolutely no way."

Her chin went up. "I'm not going to look over my shoulder and worry about my daughter's safety every day of my life. I'll meet him. Assess the threat for myself. I have a friend I'm going to enlist to come with me as backup."

"No."

"You don't get to decide for me."

"Think about your daughter. Be smart about it." It was the wrong thing to say, he realized. Inappropriate for him to offer parenting advice. Too late.

Rage kindled in her eyes and blazed across her face. "Chad Jaggert, you, above all people, don't get to tell me how to be a parent."

While he struggled with the dual urges to hug her and shake some sense back into her, a realization began to dawn in his consciousness.

You, above all people.

His mind flashed back to the picture in her silver locket.

A dark-eyed girl peeking out from under a fringe of lashes.

Dory used to tease him. *You have the thickest lashes, Chad. Wasted on a man.*

They'd been young and foolish, made some choices they shouldn't have… His palms felt sweaty. He had to be wrong. But that instinct, the one that told him when a horse was about to kick, hummed low and insistent in his gut. He went hot all over then flushed with a trickling cold. "Dory," he said slowly. "Your daughter. What's her name?"

Her swallow was audible. "Ivy."

The question spooled out as if it was someone else speaking. "How old is she?"

"Why is that—"

"How old?" he snapped.

"Almost five."

Time slowed down, lapping between them like rolling waves. His own breathing sounded loud to his ears. Five years old. Dark hair. Long eyelashes. Ivy.

His voice failed the first time, so he tried again. "Am I her father?"

She stared at him then and it didn't matter what she would say next. He read the truth in the tremble of her mouth. The lie evident, the one she'd kept for half a decade.

"Yes."

Yes. And just like that, he became a father. The incredulity of it rendered him numb. He didn't know what to do, what to say. Abruptly he turned around and stalked outside.

The spring air had a cold bite to it, yet he hardly felt it. Ivy was his daughter. The shock led him to another sizzling epiphany. All this time Dory had kept him in the dark. She'd stolen his fatherhood for years. Sucking in lungfuls of cool spring air did not stem his dizziness.

When she joined him on the porch, he was still mute.

She shoved her hands in the pockets of the barn jacket Ginny had loaned her. "I don't expect anything from you, Chad. I don't want it, in fact. She's my responsibility, and I'm taking good care of her."

He whirled to face her. "You kept my child from me."

Dory jerked before her mouth set into a hard line. "She's not your child."

"Yes, she is." Each word was a stone, flung hard at her. "I had the right to know."

Now a flush stained Dory's fair skin. "*Your* right? What were your rights exactly, Chad, after you told me you never wanted to see me again?"

He flinched.

Wind laced a strand of white-blond hair across her brow, but she didn't move to brush it away. "You turned your back on me."

"I wouldn't have if I had known…"

Again, he knew he'd said the wrong thing, but now he didn't care.

"That's exactly why I didn't tell you. If you had known," she said slowly, "you'd have stuck around me out of guilt." Tears spilled down her face. "You despised me, Chad. You blamed me for destroying your family. I wasn't about to force myself and my baby on you."

"Your baby? Don't paint this as some kind of noble act to protect me. Doesn't matter the reasons. You kept my kid from me."

Tension tightened her mouth. "I don't have to justify my decisions. You ordered me out of your life. I followed directions and left. It cost me everything, Chad, even my own family for a while." She cocked her head. "But you'd have been happy about that, wouldn't you? You would have been satisfied that I'd lost what you think I took from you." Moisture glazed her cheeks.

His own sin struck at him then, the truth in her words. He had wanted her punished; hurt, like he had been. He had desperately needed to fix blame. It hadn't been fair, but her bitter betrayal had swamped his momentary conviction.

"I want to meet my daughter," he rasped.

Instead of answering, she shouldered past him and lurched toward her car. He got in front of her as she was about to wrench the driver's door open.

She fired a tearstained challenge at him. "I'm leaving, Chad. I'm going to meet Blaze and then I'm leaving. In a matter of months we're moving to Arizona with my parents, so we won't even be in the same state anymore. It was a huge mistake to come here. I was trying to help your father, but…"

"You can't just run away now. You have to stay until we get this sorted out."

"I don't have to do anything."

He was about to snap at her when a familiar gravelly voice jabbed at him. "Son? Please tell me you're not speaking to a lady in that tone, huh?"

They both whipped a look at his father, who was standing near the hitching post, thick thatch of gray hair glinting under his battered fishing hat.

Chad looked at his fingers gripping the door handle and suddenly realized Rocky was right. He was lashing out for all he was worth at Dory. With every bit of strength he could muster, he stepped back and blew out a breath. "Sorry."

She was breathing hard, looking from Chad to Rocky. "Mr. Jaggert…"

He cracked his trademark smile, the one that somehow remained in spite of his prison time, the loss of his business and his self-respect.

"Come on now, Dory. You always called me Rocky. Don't be cluttering up the works with formalities now."

He held out his arms and Chad watched in utter befuddlement as Dory tumbled into his father's embrace.

"All right," his dad said over the top of her head. "How about we sit down and hash this out?"

Chad could think of nothing else to do but watch his father and the mother of his child enjoy a fond embrace.

In the space of a couple of minutes, his whole life had changed.

What was he supposed to do now?

EIGHT

Dory clung to Rocky for a moment, letting the familiar smell of his aftershave wash over her. He was much thinner than she remembered. Furrows grooved his forehead, and he patted her back until she pulled away. Her head spun. The explosive revelation she'd just shared with Chad beat through her.

Chad knew about Ivy. He knew he was a father. His accusation pricked her.

You kept my kid from me.

She had lied, in a sense, telling herself all the reasons why it had been the right thing to do. But now, face-to-face with Chad, she grappled with paralyzing doubt. Worse yet, she was facing another man who didn't know the truth.

Knock it off, Dory. You've done everything for Ivy. Don't second-guess yourself now.

Rocky settled into the weathered chair. Dory followed suit, taking the one next to him, catching Chad's warning look. He didn't want his father to know about Blaze until they were certain. Was it the right thing to do to tell him about his granddaughter? She had no idea. It felt as though a trap was snapping closed around her. Why hadn't she escaped the ranch a few moments earlier?

Tom Rourke ambled up the walkway, hat in his hands. "Oh, hey. Sorry, Chad. I was just coming to warn you—" He broke off as he caught sight of Rocky.

"Come on up, Tom," Rocky said. "You're too late to warn them that I heard the big news."

With a sigh, Tom leaned against a weathered beam and eyeballed Chad. "Rocky called me this morning with some gossip he'd heard in town. Made me tell him the rest."

"I was out this morning on the water." Rocky looked at Dory. "Still allowed to take out a personal craft, just not to carry any passengers."

She felt her cheeks heat for him, but Rocky, a former Marine, would never mince words, even to protect his own dignity. "Saw the police cordoning off the cave-in at the canyon. Asked around and heard a few details. Then I called Tom." He grinned. "We go back way too far for him to lie to me. Isn't that right, Tom?"

Chagrined, Tom squashed the brim of his hat against his thigh. "One of the volunteers at the cave-in was talking about… Aww, I might have misheard."

Rocky executed a massive eye roll. "The Driftwood gossip mill is turning at full speed. Tom told me someone spotted Blaze Turner."

Chad sighed. "I guess it's out now."

Tom scratched his stubbled chin. "How exactly is that possible? The Coast Guard dragged the cove for days. I tried to find him after the capsizing. We all did."

"I don't know," Chad said, "but we're going to find out."

Tom quirked an eyebrow. "Yeah? Well, that might

be a good thing, right? Maybe it will help Rocky somehow."

Rocky shook his head. "One death or two, I'll always be seen as guilty."

Tom grimaced, but Rocky stared straight at Dory and Chad. "That what you two were fussing about just now?"

Chad didn't speak, so Dory chimed in. "I'm a private investigator. I am tracking Blaze."

Rocky shrugged. "No sense in you doing that. Past is past, honey. I'm wrecked whether Blaze is alive or not."

"But if you weren't guilty, Dad," Chad said, "if someone made it look like you'd been drinking…"

Rocky's animation died in a moment and she caught the despair that cloaked him. "No one will ever believe that, son."

Chad was on his feet. "If Blaze had a hand in framing you, I'm going to prove it."

Rocky gestured to Dory. "And you're here to help restore my reputation? Because you feel guilty, right? Because you told the press I was an alcoholic? Been drinking the day before?"

Dory struggled for calm. "I didn't realize I was speaking to the press. Please believe me. I never would have…"

"Aww, I know. Your daddy drove the nails into my coffin with gusto. You were just the hammer he used to do it."

She opened her mouth to let her regret spill out, but he waved a weathered palm.

"I'm just here to tell you both to let it go. Wrecked is wrecked, but you two have lives to live. I'll get answers in due time. Leave that to me."

Alarm bells jangled in her stomach.

As Rocky struggled from his chair, Chad put an arm on his knee. "Dad, you aren't going to try to find Blaze yourself, are you?"

Rocky's gaze drifted over his son's face. "Could be I'm going to seek him out and hear what he has to say."

"Dad…"

Rocky squeezed his son's shoulder. "And I've got something to say to him, too. No matter what kind of a man he is, I let his stepmother drown." The blue of his eyes clouded and Dory noticed the trembling of his fingers. "Seems like a man owes another an apology for that kind of thing."

What could she say to dissuade him? To lift the burden that stooped his proud shoulders?

Tom lingered a moment after Rocky had cleared the door. "The guilt has eaten him up for years. He's not going to let it go. I'll watch him as best I can. Do you think Blaze has left town?"

Dory watched the indecision drift across Chad's face. Should he tell Tom of the arranged meeting? The police? There was no choice of letting the matter go now, not since it was clear that Rocky intended to do some sleuthing on his own.

Go home to Ivy, her instincts shouted. *Let the whole matter drop, just like the boulder that almost killed you.*

But there was one thing she could not deny, one more facet that she'd not allowed herself to consider before.

Rocky was Ivy's grandfather, even though he still didn't know it.

One more reason why she could not allow Blaze to vanish with answers that might provide some peace for Rocky's soul. He'd lost so much. Like he said, she'd been the hammer for her father's nails.

Chad stood with his back to her, watching Tom and Rocky walk away along the path that skirted the property. What was he thinking? What was he planning?

He crammed his cowboy hat onto his head. "I'm going to that meet tonight as your backup. If you don't want to be with me, I'll go alone. But I'm going to be there one way or another. When it's all over, we'll tell my dad what he needs to know."

Needs to know. Like the fact that he had a grand-daughter?

"I'll pick you up at six thirty. Aunt Ginny said to stay as long as you like, but if you leave, do me the courtesy of at least telling me where you are, okay?"

He didn't wait for her answer.

Dory watched his long legs eat up the ground, chin down as he left.

She'd made the right decision keeping Ivy a secret, hadn't she?

Yes, she decided, shoving the uncertainty away. Now all that remained was to solve the Blaze mystery and go back home to her little girl. She'd figure out what to do about Chad eventually.

I want to meet my daughter. His grated words rang in her ears.

One problem at a time.

Chad jerked his chin up when the clod of dirt smacked him in the chest. "What?" he growled, dropping the hammer he was using to strengthen the support for the water tank. Grumbling, he searched through the tall pasture grass to find it. Meatball and Jingles lay in the shade of an oak, tongues lolling, ever watchful.

Liam snickered. "Good thing I was lobbing dirt instead of grenades. What's eating you?"

Chad sighed. He didn't want to discuss his mountain of angst, but he knew it would be stupid to meet Blaze without some backup, and he wanted to bring people whom he trusted, not some random acquaintance of Dory's. Some level of sharing was in order. He told Liam about the meet.

"Ooookay," Liam drawled. "I'll just pretend I'm not annoyed that you didn't fill me in earlier on this dumb idea. That bridge is closed off for a reason. Unstable and isolated. Exactly the place you shouldn't meet a guy who probably threw a boulder on you."

"Not my idea, but Dory's going, and that means I am, too."

"I will have your six—you know that. Maggie's at the Lodge working extra hours anyway since Helen and Sergio took the girls to visit his folks."

Chad huffed out a breath. "And Mitch left with Uncle Gus to pick up the new baler. They'll be on the road for hours."

"I'm assuming we're going to continue our idiotic reckless streak by keeping Danny out of this?"

"Blaze says he'll bolt if he sees any interference."

Liam grinned as he loaded the extra wood and nails onto the ATV. "Then I will do my best impression of a shadow." He paused. "Anything else you want to get off your chest?"

It would do no good to avoid the question. Liam could sniff out evasion like a bloodhound on the scent. "Dory's been lying."

"'Bout what?"

"Something important she kept me from finding out from back then."

"Yeah?" He frowned. "So you contacted her after your bust-up and she withheld intel?"

"I didn't exactly contact her."

"Ahh."

Chad wiped a smear of dirt from his jeans. "What's the 'ahh' for?"

"Nothin'. I'm not exactly a relationship guru, as Maggie will tell you. Just saying that I'm coming to understand that God made plenty of gray area along with the black and white. Personally, I find that confusing, but there it is."

Gray area? A baby was certainly not a gray area. That was a thing a person should disclose under any circumstances. He realized he was grinding his teeth. "She was wrong."

Liam slapped Chad on the back. "There's a whole lot of right and wrong mixed up in that gray area I mentioned a minute ago. Annoying, but inescapable."

Chad sighed. "I've gotta get Zephyr back. I'll text you when we leave for the bridge."

"Ten-four, little brother. Secret Mission Bridge Intercept begins now."

"And if you see my dad, don't share anything. He wants to talk to Blaze. We're gonna have to keep him out of this somehow, too."

Liam laughed and got on the ATV. Jingles and Meatball immediately sprang up, ready to follow. "The Jaggert men are an ornery bunch—that's certain."

Chad considered that as Liam rode away. He'd been told on plenty of occasions that he was uncommunicative, stubborn, and rigid in his thinking. But Dory had seen better things in him, things he hadn't seen in himself. What would Ivy be like? Would she be friendly and funny, like Dory? Have his good traits? Or his bad ones?

Alone with the grass and the wind and the quiet presence of Zephyr, he finally allowed himself to dredge up the part that ached the most about Dory's revelation. Long ago, he'd made a solemn promise to God that he would never abandon a child like his mother had done. He would die before he left his progeny with the nagging uncertainty that they hadn't been worth sticking around for, worth loving. But Dory had put him in exactly that position. The sheer injustice of it made his breath catch.

What had Ivy been told about her absent father? That he'd not stuck around…that he'd not wanted her? He gulped and his common sense returned. No. Dory had always had a heart too big for her body. She wouldn't have hurt their child to repay him.

The brilliant blue sky met his eyes as he looked up. *Lord, what am I supposed to do about this mess?*

The question accompanied him back to the stables and carried right on through his afternoon work with the horses. He still hadn't gotten the smallest clue by dinnertime, and he pushed the food around his plate.

"Chad, you're gonna wither and blow away if you don't eat something," Ginny chided.

"Yes, ma'am," he said, shoveling in a bite.

"Dory staying for a while?" Uncle Gus asked.

At her name, the fork slipped from his fingers. "Yeah. For tonight, anyway."

"Well, good," Ginny said. "I'll make up a plate for you to take to her."

He did so, stomach knotted as he walked to the saddlery a couple of hours before sundown. His nerves were jangling both at the prospect of seeing Dory and the fact that his father had not answered the phone the last two times he'd called. What was he up to?

Two separate knocks and Dory didn't answer. That was when he noticed her car was gone.

Everything in him went white-hot with anger that was quickly shot through with cold fear. The plan had changed. She'd gone to meet Blaze without him.

Muscles tensed, he tried to fight through his storm of emotions.

When he'd finally decided to head for the bridge and hunt for her, her car pulled up and she got out. Relief powered through him.

"You thought I'd left," she said.

He tried to shrug it off.

Her smile was sad. "I told you I was going to stay to meet Blaze. I still keep my word, believe it or not."

He searched in vain for something to say. Five years ago, he'd trusted her with everything, including the scars left by his mother's abandonment. He'd come to find out Dory'd been deceiving him. Now he wasn't sure who she was anymore. At the moment, he wasn't sure about himself, either.

She held the handles of a paper bag. "I drove into town to buy a change of clothes so I can return the borrowed ones."

"Shouldn't drive with a busted window."

She lifted a shoulder. "I swept away the glass. Is that for me?"

He realized she meant the dinner plate.

"Uh, yeah. Aunt Ginny's meatballs."

She took the plate. "Do you…um, want to come in?"

No, he wanted to say, but something made him follow her anyway. He sat at the table while she nibbled at the meatballs, trying not to stare at the woman who was so familiar and altogether new to him.

She rolled her eyes. "Delicious. I'll have to ask for the recipe."

"Does—" He stopped. How had words starting flying out of his mouth without permission from his brain?

She put her fork down. "Go ahead and ask."

"Does Ivy like meatballs?" It had to be the dumbest question ever. His child—their child—was a complete mystery to him and he'd just asked if she liked meatballs.

After a hesitation, Dory took out her phone and pulled up a photo. It was Ivy, with spaghetti sauce all over her grinning face and a meatball speared on her fork. "Her favorite, as a matter of fact."

He stared at the picture of that happy child. Joy and anger and sadness and hurt all twined together inside. He got up and began to pace. "I don't know what to do here…about Ivy."

"I didn't, either, for a long while." The sinking sun crept through the window and painted Dory in shadow. Her tone was far-off, almost distant. "When I told my parents that I was pregnant, my father blew up and kicked me out of their house."

Chad stiffened. "He should never—"

She stopped him. "Neither Dad nor I handled things well and we've made peace with that. Anyway, rather than staying and facing it, I ran. I lived on the streets for months, in and out of shelters." She blinked hard. "I couldn't stay in my parents' house and I couldn't come back here to Driftwood. I had no idea what to do."

The knowledge made him cringe inside. He forced himself to look at her through the haze of pain. "Where did you go?"

"Anywhere and everywhere. I begged for money sometimes and slept in my car."

Bile rose in his throat. "Aww, Dory."

"God taught me plenty about humility back then. I finally landed in a church-sponsored shelter program. They were amazing and reminded me that Ivy was a gift from God. I knew I had to survive, so the baby would, too. She was the only thing I had left."

The only thing I had left. He'd felt alone after their breakup, after his father had gone to prison. He'd spent so much time nursing his wounds and, all the while, Dory had been suffering. And he'd wanted her to, hadn't he? His anger mixed with guilt and everything in between. Liam's "gray area," probably.

"The church program arranged for me to find a trailer to rent and a job waitressing. I continued on like that until I went into labor. I was scared, Chad. Barely twenty, alone and terrified. I broke down and called my mom. She and my dad came, but Ivy arrived before they did. I was alone, just me and her."

Alone.

Why didn't you call me? he wanted to say, but he knew why. "I should have been there."

She cocked her head and pushed the plate away. "I handled it."

"But I didn't get the chance even to try." Anger flicked up again and he crossed his arms. "Honestly, I don't know that I would have had the courage, but I deserved the option to be there when my child was born."

"Chad…" Her voice started out hard, but lost its edge. "Maybe. I don't know. But she's doing great. We don't…"

"Want me around? I know that's your feelings, but do you get to speak for Ivy? To decide that she doesn't get to know her father?"

Her eyes sparked. "Even if that father was a jerk to her mother?"

Again he was lost in that sea of emotions that threatened to drown him. Guilt. Anger. Pain. Regret. And why did part of him long to hold her and soothe away the terrible memories from that long-ago day? "I didn't handle things right." There, he'd said it, confessed what his heart had probably always known. "You didn't deserve to be treated like that."

Her eyes softened into that iridescent golden hue he remembered so well, the color that he would never find anywhere else on the planet.

"We both made mistakes. I—"

He did not get the chance to hear what her next words would be because her phone buzzed with a text.

She read the screen and turned it so he could see.

Here now. Leaving in 15 if you don't show.

She was already heading for the door.

NINE

Dory gripped the armrest, trying to still the butterflies somersaulting in her stomach. Chad pushed the truck as fast as was practical on the twisting mountain road. Silhouetted against the ocean, the peaks were draped with a heavy curtain of trees. The sun was gradually sinking behind a jutting rock as the road led them up the cliff side.

He turned off the paved road and onto a graveled trail that dipped into a gorge. Steep, narrow, dangerous.

The way was abruptly blocked by a chain-link fence. Beyond was a wooden bridge that spanned a hundred-foot gap from one side of the gorge to the other. Once upon a time, it had been meant for people, not cars, but the years had not been kind to the structure. The slats nailed across the bridge had warped, with dark holes indicating missing pieces. Below came the sound of a great volume of water rushing out to the ocean.

Dory had been there decades before, when she and Chad were dating. Not surprising since the spot was a teen magnet. The bridge had been rickety even back then, but it hadn't been officially barricaded until a group of boys plunged to their deaths into the water when the slats had given way underneath them.

Chad peered through the windshield at the chain-link fence. "Padlock's been cut. Liam's on his way. He'll get a bead on things as best he can. Dory..." he started, but she was already dialing her phone.

She pressed the speaker button so Chad could listen. "I'm here, Bla—"

Blaze cut her off. "Who's the cowboy?"

She realized with a start that he must be able to see them from his vantage point. No use trying to trick him. "I brought a friend."

"I told you not to."

"You shoved a boulder down on me. Alone was not an option."

Blaze went quiet for a moment. "I was trying to scare you, is all. Same reason I sent you your kid's photo."

"Yeah, about that, Blaze. If you so much as breathe in the direction of my child, there will never be a good enough spot for you to hide from me. Got it?"

Chad shot her a look that just might have been admiration. Why did that please her? she wondered.

"Whatever," Blaze grumbled.

"We're here now, like you asked. Start talking."

The phone went dead.

Dory's stomach clenched. "He hung up."

"There." Chad stabbed a finger toward a dim light visible through the chain link. "He's using his phone's flashlight to show us his position. He's right behind the gate in the shadows. Stay here."

Chad got out. He retrieved a rifle from the back seat.

Typical Chad. Full stop or full go. Never a "let's talk it over."

No, she wanted to say. *You'll spook him.* But Chad might be right. Blaze was dangerous and it would be foolhardy to seek him out unarmed. Any longer hesitation on their part might mean he'd bug out on them entirely.

"Start talking, Blaze," she heard Chad call through the fence.

So much for a friendly approach to gain Blaze's trust. She let herself out of the truck and crept closer to hear Blaze's reply.

"I'm not talking to you, man. I don't even know you. You got nothing to do with this."

The anger practically radiated from Chad. "My last name is Jaggert. Ring a bell? My dad captained the boat. You faked your death and left him to take the fall, to blame himself for your drowning all these years. And here you are, the picture of health." Chad shot Dory a furious look when she edged up next to him.

"Please, Blaze." She kept her voice calm. "We need to know what happened to you."

Blaze must have eased out farther onto the bridge. The boards creaked under his weight. "It wasn't an accident."

She must have misheard. Not an accident?

Chad jerked, shoulders rigid. "What did you say?"

Blaze's answer was lost in the gust of the wind that ripped through the canyon. Chad eased the gate open and stepped onto the bridge.

"Don't," Dory whispered, but Chad didn't reply.

"Tell us what you know," Chad said.

Blaze didn't answer.

Dory edged up behind Chad. "Why did you push the rock down on me?"

His face was a pale crescent in the darkness. "Because I thought you were working for her."

"Who?" Chad was losing patience. "Blaze, why did you come back here?"

She could not read his expression clearly, but his voice rang out like a mallet striking a gong. "The inheritance is mine. My stepmother meant it for me."

Chad tracked him with the rifle as he stepped farther out onto the worn planks. "Then why didn't you stay and claim it five years ago? Why play the possum?"

"Because she wants me dead. She sent people to track me. I've been lying low, doing what I had to do to survive, but I can't do that anymore. Time's running out and the cops are after me now, too, for the ATM job, which I didn't have anything to do with."

Dory figured it was time to negotiate. "Maybe we can help you. We have a friend in the police department."

"Cops won't believe me. No one will."

"Tell us who wants you dead."

He paused. "My aunt."

Chad darted a quick glance behind him at Dory. The woman who would profit the most from her sister's death. "Angela Robertson?"

"Yeah. She's always hated me. She—"

A shot cracked from above, striking the fence pole and sending gold sparks dancing. Blaze cried out, bolting across the bridge, stumbling to his knees.

Dory wasn't sure if he'd been shot or had fallen through a broken slat. Another shot answered immediately from below and sailed high over their heads.

Chad grabbed Dory's arm and they raced back to the truck. He pushed her into the front seat and pressed his phone into her hand. "Text Liam." He sprinted after Blaze before she could stop him.

Dory's heart thundered madly as she pulled up Chad's contacts and looked for Liam. A text appeared as she was thumbing through.

Returned fire. In pursuit. Hold your position.

She texted back.

Don't shoot. Chad and Blaze on bridge.

There was no reply from Liam. Unsure what to do, she strained to see across the darkening chasm. Her eyes adjusted in time to spot Blaze outlined in a patch of moonlight as he darted a few steps deeper onto the bridge. Chad was fifteen feet behind him.

"Don't run," Chad yelled. "Bridge isn't safe."

But Blaze seemed to have made up his mind. He jogged along the bridge, hopping over the missing slats. She got out of the truck and stepped through the gate.

"No, Blaze!" she shouted. He didn't slow.

Chad ducked down and sprinted after him.

Dory's heart shot to her throat. Their combined weight would be too much. Or the shooter would have another chance for a kill shot. Her knees trembled with the vibrations of the two running men. She had no idea how to help.

Let him go, Chad, she willed. She knew it was futile. Blaze had hinted at the knowledge that would restore Rocky's reputation. *It wasn't an accident.* No, Chad would not stop until he'd forced Blaze to reveal everything he knew. Or until one of them was killed in the attempt.

Chad was fast. He'd been an all-state sprinter until

his mother's affair with Chad's coach. Dory remembered the day he'd told her about that. It was the only time she'd witnessed him cry. The day they'd ended things, there had been no tears on his part. Just a cold, hollow fury that she still recalled in vivid detail.

"Stop!" Chad shouted again. He aimed a flying tackle at Blaze. Both men went down in a whirl of limbs that shook the bridge.

Dory clutched the railing to keep from falling.

Blaze sprang to his feet a second before Chad, who lunged once again.

Blaze dodged, twisting just enough to avoid Chad's grasp.

Breath frozen in horror, Dory saw Chad hit the railing full-force. An ominous crack cut the air.

Had it been another shot?

A second later, she realized it wasn't a gunshot but the sound of the old wood giving way.

"No," she gasped.

She bolted forward as Chad fell backward through the ruined wood.

Chad felt the railing disintegrating. An odd sense of weightlessness enveloped him, and then he was airborne, his senses on overload. Bits of wood rained down around him. He heard Dory scream. Cold air tore off his cowboy hat and whirled it away. His brain fired off a code red warning. *You're gonna wind up in the river!* At the last minute, he managed to hook an arm over a fractured beam that stuck out over the chasm. Pain shot through him as the jagged material cut into his shoulder, but he clung there, grappling until he got both arms locked around the lifesaving slab of wood. He tried to throw a leg up over the support, but he could not angle his body sufficiently. It took all his strength to hold on.

"Chad!" Dory's voice barely carried over the cacophony.

Panic drilled him as the top of her head appeared over the slats. "Get off the bridge!" he shouted. "Go back!"

Still she remained there, saying something maybe. Hadn't she heard him? "Go back!" he shouted again as loud as he could manage. He breathed a prayer of thanks when she disappeared in the direction of the truck. She'd shelter there, call the police, fill Liam in. She'd live to go back to Ivy.

The knowledge bolstered him. One problem taken care of. Next order of the day was how to survive until Liam arrived. Looking around, he saw nothing else to hold on to. Cramps seized his biceps as the wind seemed to be trying its best to pry him loose. His only chance was to try to shimmy back along the broken beam and hoist himself onto the bridge again. Judging from the way the beam shook under his grasp, it would be a one-in-a-million chance of success. At least Dory wasn't in danger of falling, too. Arms strained to breaking, he started to wriggle on the beam until another hideous crack froze him in place.

The wood shivered under his grip. Desperately, he looked for another handhold, something to support him before his perch gave way. Splinters cut into his hands and he knew he had only moments before he was going down into that water-filled gorge.

All right, he told himself through gritted teeth. *This better be the best dive of your life.* His father had never understood Chad's love of the high dive at the high school swimming pool.

At least have the good sense to go feetfirst, would you? he'd call up the ladder.

His mother used to disagree. *The water's plenty deep. Just dive, kiddo. Don't think about it too much.*

Just dive. It was the way she'd lived her life with them, diving into experiences, friendships…an affair. She plunged into everything and he'd always admired her spirit. He'd been proud of it, truth be told, until he'd finally understood the cost. Diving was a quick thrill and then what? On to the next experience, whatever would feed her, heedless of the young teen boy she'd left standing by the pool, wrecked and alone. And the husband who was left to pick up the pieces?

His father had found comfort in a bottle, and comfort had become a crutch. Chad had watched his father struggling to stay sober, sneaking drinks when he thought Chad was not aware. But it was impossible not to notice when sometimes Chad had to call and cancel charter jobs at the last minute because he could not rouse his father from yet another drunken sleep.

Nothing he could ever do would take the sting from his mother's betrayal, but with his father clinging to sobriety after his prison time, maybe Chad could find the truth. Would it be enough to set him free of the guilt that had tormented him for five years? Mary Robertson's drowning and Blaze's, or so they'd believed? He gripped the rough wood, biting back a groan of pain. Hard as he fought, his overtaxed muscles blared a warning.

Something slapped at his shoulder. A rope dangled in his line of sight.

Dory peered down at him again. "Tie it around you."

"No," he shouted up at her. "I'm too heavy. I'll pull us both in."

"I've got it fastened around the axle of your truck."

"Dory—"

"Do it right now, Chad Dooley Jaggert!"

Her shriek and the use of his full name punched through his pain. He could not abide his middle name, chosen for some folk guitar singer his mother admired, and Dory knew it. It galvanized him into action.

With one hand, he managed to grab the rope. His numb fingers struggled against the nylon.

"Hurry!" Dory's voice pitched high with panic.

I'm not exactly taking my time. He had to get the knot fastened somehow. "I've almost done it. Get back to the truck," he called to her.

Once he got the rope fastened, she could haul him up quickly using the truck. Maybe they could cut Blaze off with Liam's help. He fought against the fatigue, peeking a look. Dory was still there. She straightened, as if she'd heard something. Liam? Blaze? The shooter? His pulse raced.

He saw her knuckles whiten on the railing.

"What is it?" he hollered over the wind.

And then he felt it, too, the undulation of the bridge, the wood uncoiling like some giant snake. Too late.

"Run, Dory!"

He did not know if she'd heard him or not.

With a spine-shivering moan, the bridge collapsed. The rope slithered from his hands.

As he pinwheeled into the darkness, he watched in helpless horror as Dory was thrown into the void alongside him.

TEN

The bridge dropped away from under her feet. Spinning, twisting, limbs flailing, Dory catapulted into the chasm. There was no time to do anything but cradle her head seconds before she plunged feetfirst into the river and the ice-cold water stripped her of breath. The force of impact hit her like a sledgehammer. She could not decipher up from down. Her feet scraped against something. The bottom? And then she was propelled back to the surface only to be tumbled helplessly by the rushing current.

Chad. Where is he? Fighting the tumult, she managed to keep her chin high enough to suck in a breath before she was thrown under again. Her elbow banged against a rock. Another surge of roiling water broke over her. There was no way she was going to survive the violence much longer. She kicked with all her might, heading for a dark shadow poking up from the water. It wasn't much, a single wedge in the middle of the onslaught, but it was the only fixed point anywhere close. *Come on, come on.* She clawed her way along, but the force of the water hurtled her too far. Again she was forced under. She fought her way to the surface.

"Here."

Had she actually heard a voice? Chad? Her heart leaped.

Jerking a look to the side, she caught the barest glimpse of him holding on to a pinnacle of rock that jutted from the canyon into the raging water. Hope churned inside her. The flow would carry her right by him if only she could reach out and grab for his extended hand. If she missed, she'd be swept down the gorge and drowned or smashed to death. She tried to slow herself by snagging the rocks, but her fingers skimmed over the thick layers of slippery moss.

The water sped her along. Closer and closer she came to Chad. He was silhouetted against the moonlight, clothes plastered to his body, every muscle straining to reach her.

"Come on," she commanded herself. Coaxing her clawed fingers to extend, she reached out.

Chad grabbed her wrist and pulled her to him, defying the pummeling water. *Yes!* They were going to make it. A roaring monster of water yanked Chad from the rocks and they were both sucked along toward the narrowing walls. Chad somehow looped an arm around her waist.

Let go! she wanted to scream to him. He was a much stronger swimmer than she was. *You can make it to shore, get help.*

But he kept that iron arm fastened around her middle. There was no escape now, she knew. No rescue lay in store for them. *Oh, Chad*, she thought. *Why did I come back? What have I done to us both?* Cold pushed the thought from her mind and the breath from her body.

Moment by moment, she could feel her chance to live being sucked away by the raging tumult.

Over the roaring water, she heard a strange sound.

A bark? No, surely not. A hallucination. The deluge stripped away her last bit of strength and she could no longer hold on. Chad gripped her more tightly, but she knew his strength was waning, too. Bitter cold pushed deeper into her bloodstream.

Her daughter's impish smile danced in her mind. She considered how both Ivy's parents might well be moments away from dying together without Ivy ever so much as seeing her father. In that moment, she knew she'd made the wrong choice, keeping Ivy from Chad. He didn't love Dory, true. Maybe she hadn't forgiven him for cutting her out of his life, though she'd prayed long and hard about it. But her decision had stripped him of the chance to love his daughter. He might have been a good father or a bad one, but God had given him the title and she'd taken it away. Worse, she'd prevented Ivy from having a daddy in her world. Regret felt as bitter as the cold.

I'm sorry, Chad.

A light pierced the darkness. Chad began to struggle with fresh energy, pulling them toward the shore. Again she heard a dog bark. Rescue? Was it possible? She tried to kick, to help, but all her strength had been gobbled up by the frigid water.

"God help us," she prayed as she gave herself up to the cold.

Chad's brain was chilled into sluggishness, but the sight of that tiny beacon waving him in like runway lights revived him. Clutching Dory with one hand, he cleaved at the water with the other. His efforts didn't amount to much, but the motion veered them slightly toward the light. Dory was trying to help. Her kicks were feeble. They didn't have much longer before they both went hypothermic.

When he feared he could not continue, rocks ground at his shins. They were in shallower water. Hope fired his muscles. Straining hard, he kept at it, and suddenly Liam was there, up to his hips, tied by a rope to a tree on the bank. Chad tried to grab for him and failed. The water was sweeping them past the point of rescue. He fought to plant his feet against the mighty pull. He managed to hold for a few seconds.

It was enough. A bark sounded near his ear, and in minutes, Jingles and Meatball were in the water, too, splashing and paddling around them. He looped an arm around Jingles's neck at the same moment Liam grabbed him by the shoulder. Meatball paddled furiously, poking his face into Dory's until she lifted a shaking arm.

The little dog was not strong enough with only three legs to anchor Dory against the water, but he snatched up her sleeve in his teeth and tugged for all he was worth.

Pull, Meatball.

For a while, it seemed futile. The effort of Liam and the two dogs held them in place, but they were not moving closer to shore. Dory had gone limp. The instant Chad thought he could struggle no longer, he found himself and Dory hauled onto the mossy rocks by a panting Liam. He heaved in a massive lungful of air before he rolled onto his side and looked at Dory.

Her eyes were closed but she was breathing as Meatball licked the water from her cheeks.

"Dory," Chad breathed. "Look at me."

She didn't answer. His fingers found her face. Her skin was dead cold to his touch. He cupped her cheek. "Come back to me, Dory."

And that got a hint, the barest suggestion, of a smile. His head swam with relief. He chafed his palm up and down her arm, trying to catch his own breath and stir warmth back into her.

"These dogs never listen," Liam said, kneeling next to Dory and throwing his jacket over her. "I told 'em to stay put and what do they do? Dive right in."

Chad gulped when he saw her mouth move.

"Good dogs," she whispered.

He struggled to sit up. A jumble of feelings jetted through him just then. If Dory had not made it... The thought cut through every other emotion with a swift, hot slash. He swallowed hard against a surge of new tenderness toward her, low and insistent. No, he thought. It couldn't be a new feeling, just an echo of something long since gone. He fought the shivers and got to his knees.

Liam completed his quick exam. "I don't see obvious broken bones or bleeding."

With Liam and Chad's help, she sat up and tried to speak. "H-how...?"

Liam cocked his head. He hadn't heard her quiet murmur.

Chad squeezed her hand between his. "I think she wants to know how you managed to save us."

"Ah. That was due to my arsenal of ferocious skills," Liam said with a characteristic cocky grin. Chad could see that he was hiding concern underneath his bravado. "It will take too long to get an ambulance down here with the bridge out. I'll carry Dory to my truck and come back for you."

"I can make it," Chad said, wondering if his body would make a liar out of him. "What about the shooter?"

Again Liam hadn't heard him, so he said it louder over the sound of the thundering water.

"Couldn't get to the shooter. Laid down some fire to discourage him or her from killing you three. Saw a vehicle tearing off out of the canyon just before the bridge went down." He shook his head. "Before you ask, Blaze is gone. Dunno if he was injured or not. We will get after him at first light. I'll fill Danny in from the truck. Right now, we gotta move."

Chad made it to his feet with a hand from Liam. Liam gripped his palm for a moment, his expression earnest and fierce. "As much as I appreciate a good adrenaline rush, you scared me, little brother. How about we don't do that again, huh?"

Chad nodded. "Yes, sir. And thank you."

Liam lifted Dory easily, which set Meatball to whining, dancing on his three legs. Jingles shook off a spray of water droplets and followed after Liam.

Chad shuddered with the cold. He willed his knees not to buckle. Meatball looked up at him, sopping wet and trembling, too. He held out his arms and the dog leaped straight up into them, licking the water from his neck and snuggling against Chad's chest.

"We gonna make it, Meatball?" he murmured to the dog's wet ears. The skinny pup had risked drowning himself trying to get Dory out of the water. Unbuttoning his shirt, he cradled Meatball next to his goose-pimpled skin and made him a silent promise. However things turned out, Meatball would always have a home with Chad until the end of his days.

The steep trek to the truck felt endless. He hoped Liam did not notice his repeated stumbling. It was a cramped ride with Dory crammed into the seat between Liam and Chad, the two dogs sharing the passenger foot space. For all Liam's tough-guy attitude, he didn't want the wet dogs freezing in the truck bed. With the heater blasting, Chad noticed Dory's shivering had slowed a bit, but his worry would not be eased until she'd been given a complete exam.

Liam got them both checked in at the hospital and left to take the dogs home and alert Aunt Ginny. Dory was spirited away to some exam room while Chad was parked in another. The hospital staff ran tests, poked, prodded and checked his vitals. They would not update him on Dory's condition other than to say, "She's stable." Whatever that meant.

Danny Patron arrived to take his statement. His frown spoke volumes. "Seems like I've had similar visits with Liam and Mitch in the not-too-distant past. Tell me, is it a prerequisite that all Roughwater Ranch brothers are stubborn fools? Going off on harebrained missions without informing the police?"

"No, sir."

Danny shook his head. "That all you got to say?"

"No, sir."

Danny rolled his eyes. "What, then? Spit it out."

"Did you find Blaze?"

"No."

Chad weighed his choices about how much to divulge. "He says the boat sinking was not an accident. That his aunt's to blame."

Danny raised an eyebrow. He was dressed in jeans and a paint-splattered sweatshirt with a cartoon tiger on the front. Chad felt a stab of guilt that he'd been dragged in while off duty. "I'm looking into that. Already talked to Angela Robertson once. Gotta tell you, though, she's not hurting for money. Their folks had plenty and Angela and Mary were both doing just fine. We've done a cursory investigation, and Angela's not in debt. Far from it, as a matter of fact."

"Are you saying Blaze is lying?"

Danny got up when a nurse entered. "I'm saying we'll look more, but on the surface it would appear money is not a motive for Angela Robertson." He leaned closer, speaking low. "And she isn't the one who's been playing dead for five years."

Or threatening Dory with pictures of her child. *Their child*, he corrected before he filled Danny in on that little tidbit.

Danny had listened carefully and Chad's head pounded as he watched him leave. So, if Angela was after Blaze, she wasn't acting out of greed. But money wasn't the only motive in the world. He needed to speak to Angela face-to-face.

When the nurse left with promises to return in a couple of hours, he quickly called Liam on the bedside phone. His brother showed up twenty minutes later with a dry set of clothes.

"Uncle Gus and Aunt Ginny retrieved your truck from the bridge and snagged your phone from the front seat." He handed him his cell phone. "The room you'll be looking for is three oh seven," he said with a wink.

Chad arched a questioning eyebrow.

"Dory's room. I figured you were going to do some

reconnaissance. Ginny's on her way up to demand a full doctor's report, so you don't have much time."

Chad hadn't even got out the "Thank you" before Liam was gone. How was he always one step ahead?

He pulled on the clothes. Ignoring the network of aches in his limbs, he headed for Dory's room. He knocked, feeling suddenly hesitant, as if he was still lost in the grip of the water. He felt again the overwhelming crush when he'd thought she had not made it. Then the incredible heart rush when she'd moved ever so slightly under his touch.

The thought of a world without her nearly flayed his heart wide open. It confused him. Why? She'd been out of his life for five years. It must be because of Ivy, he told himself. He could not stomach the thought of his little girl losing her mother like he had. Right. It was all about Ivy.

As he stood paralyzed, Dory turned to face him. Her skin was pale, short hair dried in platinum waves that framed her face. A square bandage adhered to her neck. Suddenly his tongue seemed to tangle up and he wondered what exactly he'd been planning to say to her in the first place.

"The doctor said you're stable" was the best he could muster.

She smiled. "Is this what it feels like to be stable? Like I've been put through the heavy-soil cycle of the washing machine?"

"I didn't know washers had 'heavy-soil' cycles."

Surprisingly, she giggled, and it transformed her into that incandescent high school girl who'd rocked his world. He found himself holding his breath.

"That's because you dump everything in at once and hit the start button, don't you?"

He chuckled. "Yeah, I guess I do."

Silence unrolled between them and her smile faded. "Thank you. For getting me out of the water."

He shrugged. "Mostly Liam. If he hadn't come along with the dogs, we'd both have drowned." He paused. "I think Meatball has assigned himself as your life companion."

"I could do worse."

She had. With him. What was with the guilt? She'd done him and his father wrong. Nothing had changed in that regard. Had it? He hooked his thumbs in his belt loops. "Danny said Angela's got plenty of money, so the inheritance isn't a motive for her as much as it is for Blaze."

Dory frowned. "I'll look into it. See what I can find out."

"Mitch is digging, too. Liam called him."

She snagged her lower lip between her teeth. "I've been running it through in my mind. I think it would be a good idea to go through the old investigation notes in my dad's office, to reexamine the evidence from the sinking."

"You think Blaze is telling the truth? That it wasn't an accident?"

"I honestly don't know, but I'm going to check it out tomorrow if they spring me from the hospital." She paused. "I want to see Ivy, too."

His daughter. The one he'd never even clapped eyes on. Anger tightened his gut until he noticed the gleam of wetness in her eyes.

She heaved a big breath in and out. "I…I think it's time you met her."

His jaw fell open. "You do?"

She looked away. "I thought I was doing the right thing. I really did. But I now realize that maybe it was more to punish you than to take care of Ivy. I'm ashamed of that and…I'm sorry."

Still she did not look at him. The honesty of it set him back on his heels. Would he have had the courage to own such a thing? He'd been stone-cold furious for years, and only a few times had he allowed himself to consider his own brutal treatment of Dory. What kind of a man did that? He cleared his throat. "I guess I gave you reasons."

She plucked at the blanket. "I'm not sure how it will go. My dad…"

"I know." He shoved down the irritation. "We'll deal with it."

"And I don't know how the future will pan out. I mean, we've got a stable life and I don't want to upset her too much. I…"

Chad grazed a finger along her arm. Her skin was so soft, so gloriously warm, and sprinkled with freckles like bits of flaked bronze. "It's enough for now to meet her."

Her honey irises held currents of emotion that he could not interpret. Fear? And perhaps a tiny glimmer of hope? He let his touch linger for another moment, wondering if maybe he could catch hold of some of that hope, as well.

He was going to meet his daughter.

He prayed Ivy wouldn't be disappointed.

ELEVEN

Dory spent a restless night juggling thoughts of Blaze and nightmares about bullets and drowning. Mixed up in it all were thoughts of Ivy. She awoke with one memory spinning in her consciousness.

Chad's touch on her face, featherlight.

Come back to me, Dory.

The combined pain and pleasure of hearing him say what she'd craved for years made her eyes fill. Chad wanted her, but she knew it was not the truth. He'd been speaking from a place of fear, not love. That was only the silly fantasy she'd allowed herself to think about over the years when she desperately missed him. She'd given that up, given him up, or so she'd believed.

Had she made yet another mistake inviting him to meet Ivy? Their close call in the gorge had cast a new light on the situation. If she prayed to God to forgive her sins, wasn't she required to extend that same forgiveness to Chad whether or not he asked for it? And she could no longer deny her secret-keeping about Ivy had a lot more to do with anger and unforgiveness than she'd admitted to herself before. She blew out a breath.

Why was forgiveness something she craved but found so hard to offer?

Her cell phone was somewhere at the bottom of the gorge, so she'd made a call to her mother on the hospital phone. She'd not mentioned her near drowning; there was no reason to cause unnecessary worry. She'd promised to be there by late afternoon, relieved to find out her father would be away.

She didn't know exactly how he would react when she showed up with Chad, but she suspected it would not be a pleasant encounter. Best to introduce Chad and Ivy beforehand.

The release papers were finally executed close to lunchtime. She dressed in yet another set of clothes Ginny had provided: underclothes, jeans a shade too long and a gloriously soft flannel shirt. Each tug and twist shot pain through her battered body. She wondered if Chad was similarly uncomfortable. He and Aunt Ginny were waiting for her when she was rolled in a wheelchair to the hospital exit. Her body pulsed with discomfort, but she smiled at her escorts as they helped her out of the chair.

She felt the blush creep into her cheeks. "I'm so sorry..."

"To be a bother. I know," Aunt Ginny said, waving her off. "But you're not, and you're going to be feeling so much better after a hot shower and some chicken soup. Just cooked up a pot with extra dumplings."

"I..."

"Pleeeeaaaaase," Ginny said, stretching out the word. "Chad hasn't eaten a proper meal since the canyon collapse, and he was skin and bones before that. If you will join us, he'll have to put some food in his mouth out of sheer good manners. Besides, Mitch wants to talk to both of you."

Dory sighed. "To be honest, you had me at hot shower and dumplings."

She grinned. "I am nothing if not persuasive."

"That's for sure," Chad said.

Ginny aimed a glance at him. "Did you have something to add, young man?"

"No, ma'am. Nothing."

"That's what I thought," Ginny said with satisfaction.

Chad presented Dory with a new cell phone. "Programmed with our contacts and Danny's number."

She wanted to protest. Instead she took it. "Thank you."

"Anytime," he said.

An hour later, freshly showered, she eased into the chair that Chad pulled out for her. The savory steam from a bowl of chicken soup made her mouth water. Mitch absorbed the details of their adventure as they ate.

Gus shook his head. "We're gone for a few hours and you two nearly end up drowned in the river."

"Nah," Liam said. "Me and the dogs got 'em way before they went under for the third time. At the moment, Jingles and Meatball are both having an extra nap at the house. Maggie wanted to give them a proper brushing down, and I believe there are some chew sticks in the offing."

The doorbell rang. Aunt Ginny answered it, escorting Tom and a sixtysomething woman inside. Her neat chignon was caught in a barrette at the back of her neck. She wore black jeans and a cardigan thrown over a pink blouse.

Tom shifted hesitantly. "Apologies for arriving unannounced. This is Angela Robertson. She's a friend of mine and I convinced her to come and talk to you. She needs help."

"Please sit down, both of you," Aunt Ginny said. All the men stood as Angela joined them at the table, carrying with her the fragrance of floral perfume.

Angela smiled hesitantly before she fixed a look at Chad. "I am sorry to barge in. Tom told me that you saw Blaze." Her mouth twitched. "I can hardly believe I'm saying this. I already talked to the police, but Tom was insistent that I should share with you. It all seems so unreal. I've lived such a private life, it's almost painful to have to discuss it. Maybe it would be better if I spoke to you privately?"

Chad's eyes rounded in surprise. "Ma'am, all due respect, but my family knows everything about the situation. They've been trying to help untangle it all. Perhaps you wouldn't mind sharing with them, also?"

Dory was impressed with Chad's speech. She remembered him as a young teen who could hardly be heard mumbling the grace over dinner when asked by his father. Well, why not? she thought. She'd grown from a selfish teen into a mother, hadn't she? Why did it surprise her that Chad had matured just as much?

Angela glanced around the table. "All right. Is it true, that you've seen Blaze? He's alive?"

"Yes, ma'am," Chad said. He introduced Dory. "We've both seen him."

Angela huffed out a ragged breath and, for a moment, Dory thought she was going to cry. "It's just so incredible. Part of me is elated. All these years, I thought my nephew was dead. But the other part…" She trailed off.

Chad shot an uncertain look at Mitch, who cleared his throat.

"Ms. Robertson, I'm Chad's brother Mitch White-horse."

Dory noted the flick of confusion as Angela sorted through his different last name and physical appearance. Mitch was a hulk of a man, wide-shouldered, the tough-as-nails look enhanced by the scar grooving his cheek. There were no similarities between Mitch and Chad, save for the dark eyes, and less so between Chad and his red-haired, Southern brother, Liam. Mitch did not bother to explain the family dynamics. "I'm a former US Marshal, ma'am. Liam here is a retired Green Beret. We've both been assisting. What can you tell us about Blaze?"

After a moment, Angela seemed to come to a decision.

"My sister Mary met Scott Turner, Blaze's father, at a memorial service for my parents. They were killed in a car wreck thirteen years ago. Scott and my sister were married shortly thereafter. Blaze is Scott's son, technically, but Mary loved him from the first day she met him. He was twelve when they got married. His mother died from breast cancer when he was an infant, and Scott passed away from a heart attack a few months before the boating accident. He's suffered several tragic losses." Her lips thinned. "But plenty of people carry on after tragedy without…"

She accepted a cup of coffee from Ginny with a grateful nod. "Blaze was a difficult child, and Mary often didn't know how to handle him. She had little experience with kids and Scott was away on business constantly. I tried to help, but honestly, I'm no good with kids, either, especially preteens. He got wilder and wilder, but Scott wouldn't see any of it. When he got in his rages, he'd shout and break things." She shook her head. "Ruined a beautiful family portrait, one time."

Dory's heart squeezed. It must have been difficult for Angela to lose her parents and sister so close together. Families were such fragile things, she thought, struck with a pang of longing to be with Ivy.

"I tried. Mary tried. The school personnel tried. Even the psychologists—a string of them, but he had serious issues." Angela pulled the cardigan tighter around her shoulders. "I loved my sister and I would have done anything for her, anything to ease her situation, but I just couldn't think what to do."

"The boat accident—can you tell us about it?" Dory asked.

She gazed into her coffee cup. "I have a lot of guilt about that. I arranged for the fishing trip as a nineteenth birthday present for Blaze. He'd been calmer, making plans to move out even, and I thought it would be a show of goodwill. If I had known…" She squeezed her eyes shut for a moment. "Mary joined them at the last minute." Her gulp was audible. "I lost my sister in that accident and I thought my nephew, as well."

Dory saw Chad stiffen. She put a hand on his arm to restrain him.

He pulled away. "My father wasn't drinking that day. Blaze said the accident was staged."

Angela's mouth opened in surprise. It seemed an eternity before she spoke. "I understand not wanting to accept what happened. I didn't want it to be true, either, but Mary drowned and your father was in charge of her safety. That's an undeniable fact."

Chad's eyes glittered. "Maybe the facts aren't what they seem to be."

Angela cocked her head. "My sister is dead. That's a detail you can't change."

Chad's mouth pinched as Angela continued.

"But one thing I know for certain is that Blaze has come back after all these years for a reason."

Mitch raised an eyebrow. "What reason is that, ma'am?"

"To kill me," she said.

Chad wanted to be angry at Angela for her blunt remarks, but he couldn't be. She believed, the same as everyone else, what Dory's father had helped prove. Rocky was guilty. Blood alcohol levels didn't lie. He gritted his teeth. *Your job now is to listen.*

Fear enhanced the creases around her mouth. Tom put a hand on her shoulder.

Uncle Gus frowned. "Has he made threats, Miss Robertson?"

Aunt Ginny handed her a tissue box. She extracted one. "Call me Angela. There have been certain things happening, bad things, which I chalked up at first to accidents. My horses were let loose. Tom had just delivered a new mare and he secured the gate, yet the horse was wandering by the road when we found her. As I was trying to bring her back, a car almost ran into me."

"She couldn't make out the driver, and that gate was locked good and proper, by the way," Tom said.

Chad didn't doubt Tom's word. If he said the gate was closed, that was enough for Chad.

"There were broken windows. Looked like someone tried to force the kitchen door lock and it appeared like someone was trying to tamper with her brakes, but she refused to believe me. I finally convinced her to talk to the cops just this week," Tom said. "She's already spoken to Danny today and explained everything, but when I heard Blaze arranged to meet you at the gorge, I figured we should all get on the same page."

Dory's brow furrowed. "But what would Blaze gain by killing you? Do you think this is about the inheritance?"

Angela sighed. "No doubt. The irony is I would have been happy for him to have Mary's portion, just like she intended for him. I don't need the money. Mother and Dad were well-off, and I've never wanted for anything." She heaved out a breath. "He would squander it, I have no doubt. That would have killed my father to see it."

"Why would he need to threaten you, then?" Mitch leaned forward. "Isn't he the inheritor of his mother's estate just by virtue of his still being alive?"

"Certainly, but she and Scott were liberal spenders. There's not an exorbitant amount of Scott's money left for him. Our family money, on the other hand, is a far bigger pot. Mary put her portion aside in a trust for Blaze. He gets access when he's twenty-five upon the event of her death. Like I said, he was welcome to it."

Liam crushed his napkin into a ball. "Which is why he's turned up again before he's declared legally dead, but why doesn't he go to the police? That's what innocent people do—they go to the cops. He should be speaking up for himself. 'I'm not dead after all, so can I have my share in the Robertson estate, please?' Done deal."

Dory chimed in. "The police want to question him

about an ATM robbery. He could be afraid he'll be arrested."

"Still not a motive to go after his aunt," Liam said.

Tom cleared his throat. "I think his motive isn't just to claim his portion. He doesn't get along with Angela, and…well, if she dies, he gets her share, too."

Dory considered this new angle. With Angela alive, he would get a nice settlement, his stepmother's share. With Angela dead, he was loaded for the rest of his life. "Angela, he alleged you sent people to kill him."

Angela massaged her temple. "He's unstable. He always has been, and he has this incredible way of deflecting blame. His therapists suggested he has narcissistic traits and, on top of that, he's amazingly persuasive. He can make anyone believe it's not his fault—teachers, his parents. Somehow he's always the victim."

Chad cocked his chin at Dory. "Might explain why he wanted to meet up with you. If he thinks Angela hired you to track him down, he's got reason to find out what you know or kill you outright to get you off his track."

A ripple of cold trickled down Dory's spine as a realization dawned. "Or he doesn't want me looking deeper into that boat accident now that he's come back for his inheritance." She saw Angela shift uneasily. "Is there something you want to say about that?"

Angela blanched. "I…I didn't even really let myself think it until you brought it up a moment ago."

"Think what?"

Angela frowned.

Tom nodded. "It's okay, Angela. They're good people. You can tell them."

The room went dead still.

"Is it possible Blaze secretly invited his mother along on that fishing trip because he knew the boat was going to sink?"

The horror of her statement made Chad catch his breath. "You're saying Blaze somehow arranged for the accident to kill his mother?"

Angela didn't answer for a moment. "I don't know how he would have, but the thought just occurred to me. There's a stipulation in the trust that he gets access at an earlier age if he was to become orphaned. Maybe he wanted her dead so he could get the money early."

"And something went wrong. He decided to run until things died down?" Mitch put in.

Angela shook her head. "But it sounds so far-fetched. Blaze loved Mary. I didn't get along with my nephew, but I never questioned his love for her. I'm sure that was sincere. Could he actually have murdered his mother?"

"Stepmother," Tom corrected.

Angela shook her head. "Mary was the only mother he remembered. He loved her. That theory can't be right. He wouldn't have murdered her, even to get access to his trust early."

"I've worked enough private-eye cases to know that people are capable of just about anything, especially where money is involved. 'Follow the money' is the core of any solid investigation," Dory said.

"We'll find out what we can," Mitch said. "But I'd urge you to tell Danny Patron about your suspicion."

Chad was silent, brows drawn together as Aunt Ginny walked Tom and Angela out.

"What are you thinking?" Dory asked.

"For all these years, I've wanted nothing more than to hear what she just said, that someone framed my father.

Now both Blaze and Angela have hinted at it." He shifted to ease the muscles in his shoulders before he turned his gaze on her. "Is there actually a chance that we can clear him?"

Dory reached out and covered his hand with hers. "If there's a way, I'll help you find it, no matter what."

His gaze roamed her face. "We'll work together, then." Would she decline? Tell him she didn't want him involved after what had happened between them? He couldn't really blame her.

Her voice was low and soft. "All right. We'll work the case together."

The case…and they'd have to sort out what to do about Ivy. Together. The notion felt odd, like taking off a heavy winter coat to welcome spring. Odd…and frightening.

Don't get any ideas. Dory's not looking for anything but a practical partnership and neither are you.

He surveyed the expressions around the table and the nagging problem she'd momentarily buried bobbed up. "There's just one thing, of course, that doesn't fit with either Blaze's or Angela's story."

Mitch nodded. "Who was the shooter at the gorge?"

An enemy of Blaze's who'd followed him to town? Or someone already there who was determined to stop any questions about what had happened five years ago?

TWELVE

"Slow down."

Chad blinked and eased off the gas, noting Dory's hand clutching the armrest. "Sorry. I was lost in thought." That didn't quite capture it. His brain was wrangling with the evidence that had been collected against his father, primarily by Dory's father, Pete. But as the miles passed by, his thoughts kept drifting to Ivy. The more he thought of her, the tighter his stomach knotted.

Ivy. His daughter. What was he going to say? He'd never had to work hard to make conversation with Mitch and Jane's son, Charlie. As long as he could build block towers and chug a toy train around a track, there hadn't been much need in the way of conversation. That suited Chad just fine. Now he worried his tongue might be permanently adhered to the roof of his mouth.

"Do you want to…um…talk about it?"

"No," he said, not looking at her.

"All right. But just so you know, I'm not going to tell her you're her dad. Not yet."

Remnants of his earlier anger sparked to life. "Why not? It's the truth. Why shouldn't she know I'm her father?"

"Because," she said patiently. "She's young and it would be too much of a shock to introduce her to a total stranger and say, 'Hey, Ivy. This is your daddy.'"

He couldn't deny the logic in it. She knew these kinds of things because she'd been a mom all this time. "Oh, right."

"I will tell her, when the time is right, after a few visits."

He slowed to let a squirrel dart across the road. "How did you learn all that?"

"Learn what?"

"How to do all the parenting things?"

She sighed. "On-the-job training. Long nights, lots of mistakes."

Mistakes. He went cold. What if he said something wrong? Upset her? Broke her trust like some horses he'd dealt with that'd had rotten owners? Kids had to be way more savvy about their caretakers than horses. She'd see he didn't know what he was doing, imagine that he didn't like her, didn't want her. Be ashamed of his worn jeans and beat-up truck. Cold sweat beaded on his forehead. What if he messed up the job of parenting like his mother had?

He realized he was clutching the steering wheel in a death grip when she touched his shoulder.

"Chad, it's going to be okay. Ivy is a wonderful child." She paused. "She's got a lot of you in her."

Him? He goggled, gulped and squirmed on the seat. "That scares me. I was hoping she took after you."

Dory laughed then; a robust peal of joy that he wished he could hold on to and listen to again when he wasn't so scared. "Well, she doesn't talk much, so that's definitely a Chad trait."

His daughter didn't talk much. That made him breathe a little easier. Chad was comfortable with silence. Quieter than a fly on a feather duster, as Liam was fond of saying.

They pulled up at a small house set back on a neatly tended square of grass. A pristine white fence enclosed the teeny yard.

A Rental Property Coming Soon sign hung on a stake. He jerked a look at her. "When are you relocating?"

"We're moving to Arizona next month. My dad is retiring there, and the cost of living is cheaper."

He wasn't sure how to react. He was upset to think of her taking Ivy away, but he hadn't even clapped eyes on the girl. A week ago, he wouldn't have cared where Dory lived. Now…

His thoughts were derailed when he recognized Dory's mother, Sarah, standing in the yard. A small girl was pouring dirt into a clay pot. Long hair, slender, freckled. Ivy. Now he was sweating full-out.

Dory let herself out of the truck while he experienced momentary paralysis. Before she shut the car door, she leaned in. "Ivy's staying with my parents this week, but Mom brought her over so she could take care of her garden. She's really into plants."

A plant lover, like Dory. The best present he ever gave her was a box stuffed full of seed packets he'd found on a shelf in the boathouse where he'd worked part-time during the school year. She'd absolutely squealed with delight, immediately making plans for a summer vegetable garden.

"Chad?"

It dawned on him that he was staring, so he forced

himself out of the vehicle and into the yard. He thought he might shake Sarah's hand, but she wrapped him in a hug instead. "It's so good to see you."

Sarah would have been his mother-in-law if things hadn't gone so terribly wrong. And Sarah was Ivy's grandmother. She'd known all along, too, that he'd had a child, and she'd helped Dory keep the secret from him. He wanted to be angry about it but, for some reason, he wasn't. Hadn't been her secret to tell.

She spoke in a whisper. "I'm sorry things are working out this way, but I'm glad you're going to meet her. It's what I've been praying about for quite a long time."

Dory had already swept Ivy up in a big hug, kissing her cheeks until she squealed. "I want you to meet someone. This is Mr. Jaggert."

Yep. His tongue had definitely become glued to the roof of his mouth. He barely remembered to snatch off his cowboy hat and extend his palm. "Chad. Uh, my name's Chad."

Ivy gave him a smile that crinkled her nose the exact same way Dory's did. Her hand was so small in his, so smooth and fragile, like a tiny baby bird he might hurt with a careless squeeze.

"Pleased to meet you, sir," Ivy said, confounding him with her grown-up manners.

"Uh, yes. I am…er, pleased, too," he mumbled.

Her voice was itty-bitty, but her grin was bigger than life. Dory's smile. His eyes. It took his breath away. The silence grew awkward. "What are…? I mean…what are you growing in your garden?"

Dory put her down, and Ivy walked to her crooked row of pots. He shot a scared glance at Dory, who urged him to follow with a flutter of her hands. He did, and

Ivy told him about her newly sprouted lettuce, tomato plants and the tiny new pumpkin seedling.

Pumpkin. The word was like a conversational life jacket. "I live on a ranch, and my aunt Ginny grows pumpkins. Sometimes they get big around as barrels." That widened Ivy's inky eyes. It thrilled him to have interested her. He looked at Dory, who gave him a thumbs-up.

They talked for a while about this and that. Mostly he listened and even helped hold a clay pot while she crammed in an apple seed she'd carefully extracted from a pocketed napkin.

Sarah took in the soiled knees of her granddaughter's jeans. "Okay, Ivy. Time to get you some clean clothes and pop over to the office to see if Grandpa Pete will be home for dinner." She raised an eyebrow. "You are invited to join us for dinner, Chad." There was a glimmer of steel in her expression. "It's about time to get our family ducks in a row, and Pete is going to have to understand that, especially now."

Though Dory's face went a shade paler, she nodded. "Yes. It's past time, I'd say."

Sarah's mouth crimped. "Are you two...back together?"

Back together? He saw Dory's cheeks turn rosebud pink. An image of them standing on that tiny front porch watching their daughter play teased his imagination. But no, they weren't dreamy teenagers anymore. They were two people who'd betrayed each other. A boy and a girl who'd grown into a man and a woman. They weren't a couple.

He finally settled on something to say. "I'm helping out with an investigation. That's all."

Dory looked away, as if he'd said something distasteful. But that was the truth, wasn't it? He didn't want anything deeper than a cooperative partnership and time to get to know his daughter. Did she want something more? Did he?

But the moment had passed. Dory kissed Ivy and bundled her into her car seat in her mother's vehicle.

"I'll come by the house soon, I promise."

Ivy wriggled in her car seat. "Will Mr. Chad come, too?"

Dory didn't look at him. "Uh, maybe. We'll see."

Sarah drove off.

The uncomfortable confusion enveloped him. Should he go to the house? Be content to revel in his first precious moments with his child? Or make an excuse and press for another more private invitation? Aunt Ginny constantly reminded them that giving thanks was the most important step in any knotty decision. God had made him a father and introduced him to his girl. He let out a deep breath. "Thank you for letting me meet her."

Dory nodded, eyes damp. "I'm sorry it took me so long."

I'm sorry I sent you away, he wanted to say. As he was getting up the courage, his phone rang. He answered.

"Hey, man," Liam said. "Just now checked my messages and I got one from Tom. He said Rocky borrowed his car." He paused. "To go to Pete Winslow's office and demand a look at the case file. I think he's trying to figure out how to find Blaze."

Chad's heart dropped to his boots. What was his father thinking? Coming here? Now? He had to intercept Rocky before World War III erupted. "When did he leave?"

"Thirty minutes ago, I gather."

Chad hung up with a groan.

Dory was staring at him. "What?"

"My dad is on his way to talk to your dad about Blaze."

Dory gasped. "Oh, no."

He yanked the keys from his pocket. "Where's his office?"

Dory jogged behind him to the truck. "Twenty minutes from here. This isn't going to go well."

"I know. I just hope we get to your father before my dad does." Facing Pete Winslow, the man who thought of Chad and his father as one level above pond scum, wasn't going to go well, either. His tension ratcheted up with each stoplight.

As they rolled up, his breath hitched. Tom's Suburban was parked in a slot outside a neatly painted office building with Winslow Investigations painted in gold lettering. The shouting was audible from the lot as they raced inside.

Pete stood with hands steepled on his desktop. His face was fuller than Chad remembered, his gray hair thinner. The eyes were the same, though, blazing fury at Chad's stone-faced father.

"I've done my time, Pete. What's it going to hurt to show me the files? You got what you wanted. I went to prison, didn't I?"

"You deserved to be there," Pete stormed.

"Stop, Dad," Dory cried.

Chad stepped to his father's side.

"I'm looking out for you, Dory. Rocky killed two people."

"No, he didn't," Dory snapped.

"What are you talking about?"

She squared off with him. "Blaze is alive. We need to look at your files again, to reexamine the case notes."

Pete's gaze swiveled to Rocky. "I'm not showing him anything."

Chad's blood burned. "So you're still trying to deny my father justice?"

"I delivered justice. He got what he deserved. Now you and your sorry excuse for a father can leave my office and stay out of our lives."

Chad jerked forward. Rocky gripped his shoulder.

"He's not going to do that," Sarah answered from the doorway, startling them all.

"Mom?" Dory gasped.

Sarah stepped toward her husband, Ivy's hand tucked in hers. She bent to talk to the child. "Would you go get Grandma a bottle of water from the fridge in the back room?"

Ivy nodded and scooted off. Sarah straightened.

"There will be no more of this. Whatever feud you two concocted years ago is done." She glared at her husband. "I married you, Pete, and that should be enough to squash any rivalry. We aren't twentysomethings anymore and I'm done with this whole business."

"I don't want my daughter mixed up with the Jaggerts," Pete said. "They're—"

"Stop, Dad." Dory's mouth pinched in a hard line. "These men are important to me. Rocky's been punished, and you used me to help with that. But it's done. I won't be party to hurting them anymore."

Her voice cracked and Chad longed to reach out to her.

"He's…" Pete started to say, but a glance between

his wife and Dory took his words away. Chad heard his teeth grind together.

Ivy returned and handed her grandmother the bottle of water. Wide-eyed, she looked at the angry faces gathered around the desk.

Dory seemed to grow a little taller as she spoke. "You and Rocky are going to cooperate because of Ivy. We're family."

The room went dead quiet as Rocky looked hard at the child. Then his gaze drifted to Chad, who gave him a subtle nod. Realization dawned.

"Ivy," Dory said softly, "this is another Mr. Jaggert. He's Chad's father. I'd like you to get to know him."

Your other grandfather. It was another moment that left Chad speechless.

"Why is everyone mad?" Ivy asked.

The question cut right through Chad, but he couldn't think of how to reassure her.

Rocky blinked. He slid off his cap and twisted it between his hands. "I, uh… I'm sorry to be arguing here with your grandpa. It wasn't polite to fuss in front of you. My apologies." Solemnly he held out a hand to Ivy and she shook it.

"It's okay." Ivy rubbed her nose. "Do you want to see the sunflowers Papa let me plant back at the house? They're gonna tip toward the sun when they get bigger, Mama says."

Rocky blinked. "Um, well…" He shot a glance at Sarah, who gave him a firm nod. "Sure I would."

"Great," Sarah said cheerfully. "We'll go see those sunflowers and I'll make some lemonade. Pete, please join us when you can." And she sailed out with Ivy.

Chad's father shrugged and followed. Chad figured he now knew where Dory got some of her inner steel.

All right. If she could handle herself, he'd try, as well.

"Mr. Winslow, I apologize for us barging into your office, but Blaze is alive and he's made threats against your daughter and possibly his aunt," Chad said.

Pete blanched. "Threats?" His worried glance flicked over Dory and she nodded. "The aunt's name is Angela Robertson, correct?"

"Yes, Dad. Why?"

"Because I got a message on the machine this morning from an Angela Robertson wanting to meet with me."

Dory's brows arched in surprise.

Chad felt the same, but he forged ahead. "I know we've got some bad road behind us, but we both want Dory safe, so I'm asking for your cooperation."

Pete looked at the top of his desk. "I've never liked you, Chad."

Chad's chin went up a few inches. "I know. I'm not asking for your approval, just your help."

Pete released a long, slow huff. "That file is in the storage room. I was going to go over it with Angela when she arrived later today." He grabbed his jacket from the back of the chair. "I have to go give an affidavit at the courthouse. I'll make some calls from the car on my way to see if I can find out anything."

"Thank you, Dad," Dory said.

His face softened for a moment. Then he turned to Chad. "I'm doing this for Dory and Ivy."

Chad met Pete's stare. "Me, too."

A long, silent moment passed between them and Chad felt as if there was some sort of détente formed in that space of time, at least temporarily. Pete walked out. A car engine fired to life in the front lot and he drove away.

Dory blew out a breath and sagged against the door-jamb. Tears sparkled in her eyes. She looked so small and exhausted. Two scratches on her neck served as a reminder of their terrifying experience in the gorge. She'd been juggling so much, trying in that earnest, fully committed way of hers to make everything right. Without thinking, he pulled her close and kissed the top of her head. She fit as perfectly as he remembered in his arms, her crown of hair ticking his chin.

"I'm sorry," he said. "I know that was uncomfortable."

"It's partly my fault. I've made a mess of things," she mumbled into his chest. "I thought I was being a good mom doing everything myself, but seeing Rocky's face, and yours, knowing you missed out on…" Her tears wet his shirtfront.

He tipped her chin up and his resentment faded away as he sought to comfort her. "You've raised an amazing daughter and you endured all the hard times by yourself. I probably wouldn't have done a very good job in the parenting department anyway. I was so angry, and I let that take over my life. It would have spread to Ivy's, too. You're a good mom, Dory. I just hope I can be as good a dad."

Her smile was so radiant then, as if he'd just given her the Hope Diamond. He could not resist pressing a kiss to her mouth. The gesture was light and sweet, an impulse to comfort perhaps. But it sent through him the most tender longing, a sense of peace and wholeness that he hadn't felt ever, even on the eve of his intended proposal. The impulse bubbled out before he thought it through. "Maybe you don't have to move." He rushed on. "We can start over, you and me."

She jerked back, staring at him. "Become a couple again?"

"Yes. It would be the best thing for Ivy."

He felt her tension, but he didn't understand it. "What's wrong?"

"Don't suggest getting back together just because you know we have a child."

"Isn't that a good reason?"

"Yes, but it's not enough."

He tried to figure out how to fix whatever he'd said. The words eluded him.

She continued before he could come up with anything.

"You stopped loving me five years ago. Your feelings haven't changed since then, have they?" Her voice was tremulous and earnest.

"That doesn't matter. We have a child. It's my job to help raise her."

"Your job?" Her lip quivered. "Duty is not a good foundation for a marriage."

He fisted his hands on his hips. "It's what a dad is supposed to do. I can get us a place so you wouldn't need to move away. Help with the costs and—"

"Ivy and I don't need you," Dory blurted.

He felt something inside slam shut at her tone. He stepped back.

"I meant…" she began.

"Pretty clear what you meant."

"Chad—"

He cut her off. "We'd better find that file."

She wiped her face with her sleeve and walked down

the hallway toward the back of the building. He fell in behind her.

You stopped loving me five years ago.

It was true. But for a moment there, lost in that kiss, he thought he might have felt the flicker of a new kind of love kindling in his heart. He'd tried to express it in his growing desire to take care of them both, but she clearly didn't want anything from him, not care, nor affection, nor anything deeper that he might dream up.

Ivy and I don't need you.

Six words had quenched whatever fantasy he'd imagined.

Bitterness tugged at his heart. They weren't meant to be a couple. He'd solve the case for his father and keep the mother of his child safe.

End of story.

THIRTEEN

A cold weight settled in Dory's chest even as her lips still tingled from Chad's kiss.

Ivy and I don't need you. She regretted having to say it, but she could not allow Chad to delude himself into pretending they could be a couple because she'd had his child. It would only lead to resentment in the end. Better to go it alone than to enter into a relationship born of duty or guilt.

The rotten thing was that she couldn't escape the strange emotions that had started prickling to the surface the moment she'd seen Chad back at the canyon. She had the sneaking suspicion she might even be falling in love with him all over again. No, she thought, biting her lip. Those feelings were smoke from a long-ago fire, memories of an intense relationship, her first love.

That was why her heart beat faster when he was near. Sentimentality about the past. Again she thought of the kiss, and her somersaulting senses refused to be still. How was she going to navigate the parenting waters with a man who evoked such confusion in her? "One thing at a time," she mumbled savagely.

Chad spoke from behind her. "What did you say?"

"Nothing." She opened the door to a small, window-less storage room no bigger than a walk-in closet. Tucked inside were two upright drawers filled with older files. Though Dory had eventually convinced her father to transition to a computer, Pete Winslow kept his old-school setup. The tight space required them both to crowd inside and all but close the door to open the file drawer.

She located the one she needed, the file Angela was eager to see, as well.

Jaggert, R.

Opening the manila folder, she scanned the contents while Chad eased closer. His shoulder touched hers and again her pulse ticked up a notch.

Blinking hard, she refocused, resolved to solve the case before her emotions got any more muddled.

She thumbed a page. "Here's the invoice for the fishing excursion. It confirms that Angela booked the trip for Blaze. There's no mention of Mary joining in, except for a handwritten note at the bottom indicating she arrived at the last minute, paid cash.

"It squares with what Angela told us, but then again, it could support Blaze's story, also. If Angela somehow arranged the accident to kill Blaze, she would have made sure her sister was not aboard."

Chad frowned and traced a finger along the paper. She tried not to register the clean smell of soap that clung to him. "Angela said Blaze caused the sinking in order to kill his mother. Maybe he persuaded Mary to join him at the last minute? I still don't see how the thing could have been done."

Chad was reading ahead on the next page. "There's the information about the blood alcohol levels and such, and Dad's testimony that all he'd drunk that day was coffee from his thermos."

The thermos had never been recovered.

"How would he not have tasted the alcohol?"

Chad sighed. "Vodka doesn't have a strong taste and my dad drinks coffee dark enough to peel paint, plus he adds sweetener and cream."

She mulled it over. "Even if the thermos had been found and it contained alcohol, Rocky could have put it there himself. It wouldn't have cleared him unless there were other fingerprints found on it." She felt his tension. "I know you dived that area for weeks looking for it."

"So did the police and Coast Guard divers. We all figured it had been swept out to sea." He went quiet.

She knew he was lost in the details of that night. The boat had overturned in the Driftwater Cove when a rogue wave hit, cracking the windshield and flooding the cabin where Mary and Blaze had been. Though he could not recall specifics, Rocky had testified that, to the best of his recollection, he had been at the back of the boat, tending the fishing gear. He'd been thrown overboard but managed to cling to a bucket that went over, too. It had been a cloudy day, with a storm threatening to arrive later. Visibility was poor. They were about ready to head back to the docks when the accident occurred.

Tom Rourke had checked in at the dock with a supply of bait for Rocky, but he'd been running late and missed the boat. He borrowed a motor skiff to intercept, but when he'd finally found *The Second Wind*, it was overturned, Mary and Blaze missing. He'd called the Coast Guard, but it had been too late to save anyone but Rocky.

"My dad said it should have been him that died."

Chad still sounded as though his mind was caught up in that awful day. He sighed. "I'm afraid the stress of this whole thing is going to make him start drinking again. He got sober in prison, but…"

She had known his father's alcoholism was the greatest stressor in Chad's younger days. How many times had he excused himself from their dates, finding reasons to swing by his house? She knew it had been a cover story so he could check on his father. She'd found Chad one time, head in his hands on the tiny front porch, face bleak. Inside, an inebriated Rocky was singing some tuneless song.

I canceled Dad's charters for the day, Chad had said, mouth tight. *Dunno how we're going to cover the bills this month.*

I can help, she'd said quietly.

Wrong thing to say.

We don't need charity, he'd immediately snapped, the humiliation written across his face. *Gus said I can have extra hours at the ranch.*

And working at the Roughwater included a few meals, too. She'd been horrified when she'd learned that the cookies she'd baked in Home Economics class had served as Chad's breakfast and lunch for a couple of days after his dad drank away their grocery money. After that, she'd regularly made up excuses to try out recipes that would conveniently result in plentiful leftovers for Chad and Rocky.

The pain in his voice was too much. She turned and put her palm on his chest. "We're going to find answers if there are any to be found." At the very least, Rocky might find comfort when they proved without a shadow of a doubt that Blaze had survived the accident.

He half smiled and shifted until he broke the connection between them.

Ivy and I don't need you. Another helping of pain she'd meted out. Clearing her throat, she turned to the section about Blaze.

There was a photocopied picture of Blaze as a preteen, standing between a smiling Mary and Scott Turner. It was the same one that had circulated directly after the accident. She still remembered the headline: *Boating Under the Influence Causes Death of Mother and Stepson.* She'd tried to get close to Rocky or Chad at the trial, to tell them how sorry she was, but they'd been surrounded by lawyers and press. The one time she'd locked eyes with Chad across the courtroom, he'd swiftly looked away, as if having her around caused him physical anguish.

Maybe it still did. He increased the space between them.

"Let's go back to the office. More room."

"Sure." A strange smell froze Dory in her tracks. "Chad, is that smoke?"

His fingers reached for the slightly opened door when it was abruptly pulled closed. He went for it again, but this time something was wedged underneath that made it catch. Smoke trickled under the threshold in a thickening cloud.

Chad attacked the door again, kicking at whatever had wedged it shut. What she'd seen over his shoulder through the slightly opened door made her want to scream. A wall of smoke, the orange flicker of flames. The entire hallway was ablaze.

Chad threw himself against the wood with all his might, but whatever was holding it stuck tight. They were trapped.

Chad moved her to the back of the storage room. "Get down on the floor, where the air is cleaner."

He crouched next to her and dialed his phone. "You call 9-1-1 while I try to get my father."

Acrid smoke stung her nostrils as she dialed, choking out her message to the dispatcher.

"My dad's not answering. I left a voice mail." He scanned the room.

"No exits," she said, eyes streaming now. "Only the door."

"The fire department will be here soon."

Not soon enough. She felt as if she was already suffocating on the noxious fumes. "Wait. There's an attic access."

"Smoke's gonna rise into the attic, too."

"But there's a window there. It's small, but it opens into the rear parking lot. We stored some of Ivy's Christmas presents up there last year."

He was already on his feet, shoving the file cabinet out of the way to get to the framed three-by-three cut-out in the ceiling. He pushed the panel aside and hauled down a wooden ladder. Taking the rungs two at a time, he disappeared. A moment later, his face reappeared above her. "Come up."

Racked by coughs, Dory stumbled up the ladder. Her feet slipped and she almost fell, but his hand shot out and gripped her wrist, steadying her the rest of the way.

The attic beams were partially covered by plywood in the center, home to some dusty storage boxes. It was stiflingly hot and sweat trickled down her spine as she crawled after Chad to the window.

Muscles straining, he tried to lift it open, but it was stuck fast. Instead he kicked through the glass with his boot and cleared away the remaining shards.

"You can crawl out. It's about a fifteen-foot drop,

but there's a drainpipe. Remember how you used to shimmy up and down that rope in Phys Ed class? Everyone called you Cliffhanger after that."

She returned his smile with a shaky one of her own. "I remember."

"Okay. Time to strut your stuff, Cliffhanger."

She scooted feetfirst through the empty window frame while he held her wrists. Outside, she dangled there for a stomach-dropping moment while her feet flailed for purchase.

"I got a foothold," she told him jubilantly. "The drainpipe feels solid enough to hold both of us."

He gave her a thumbs-up through the smoke. "You go on down. Run away from the building, okay?"

It was at that precise moment when she realized the terrible reality.

Chad could not fit through the small window.

He was trapped inside.

Chad could hardly see her through the smoke, but he felt her reverse direction.

"No," he said, pushing her away. "Go down, Dory. Right now."

Her eyes were wide through the veil of smoke. "I'm not leaving you here."

He barred her way back through. "Fire department will be here any minute, and I've got fresh air via this window. Go down."

Her voice hitched. "No, Chad."

He grabbed her hand and pressed a kiss into the palm. Again he marveled at how she could be both delicate and strong at the same time. "Get along with you, Cliffhanger. I'll be all right."

"Chad…"

"Can't risk both of us, honey," he said as gently as he could. "Ivy needs her mother."

Tears crowded her eyes. "She needs her father, too. What I said before—"

He leaned through the window and stopped her with a kiss. He knew he shouldn't have, but if he wasn't going to make it out of that attic, he wanted her to remember that he'd loved her, once upon a time. That he believed in her. "You're a great mom, Dory. Now go." He all but shoved her back out onto the drainpipe.

He could barely make out a couple of vehicles speeding up into the parking lot, but neither came with the coveted red lights and sirens. The heat was nearly unbearable, and he pressed his face to the gap, trying to feel a whiff of cool air. He craned his neck to catch sight of Dory safely on the ground. Had she gotten away?

He would have gladly leaped straight out that window if he could have squeezed his shoulders through. The important thing was that Dory had made it. A siren squealed in the distance as he fought dizziness. He pulled his shirt over his mouth to filter the smoke, but it was thick now, filling the corners of the attic. Most people who died in fires didn't burn to death, Mitch had told him. They died from smoke inhalation. He climbed back toward the ladder and lurched his way down, vowing to try once more to force the door open. His vision began to go fuzzy.

His throat was dry as he recalled Aunt Ginny's advice about gratitude.

God, thank You for letting me meet my daughter, he thought as he drifted into unconsciousness.

FOURTEEN

Dory clambered down the drainpipe through a haze of smoke. She half ran, half staggered. "Someone please help." Rocky seized her by the arms. His eyes were wide with fear.

"I got the phone message. Where's Chad?"

She coughed with such violence she could not answer. A rescue engine roared up. Two firefighters leaped out and hooked up to a nearby hydrant. An ambulance screamed in behind them.

"He's…" She started coughing again.

Rocky's fingers dug into her arms. "Where, Dory?"

Desperately, she jabbed a finger upward. "Attic."

Rocky let her go so suddenly she fell to one knee. He ran toward the office building. As he got close, an arriving police officer snatched at his arm. "You can't go in there, sir."

"My boy's trapped inside," Rocky thundered, but the cop held him tight.

The firefighters dragged a hose closer to the building. She could not see flames, but smoke was still billowing into the air. Her mouth and nose burned.

Chad. Chad. His name echoed with every thrum

of her pulse along with her hurtful words. *Ivy and I don't need you.* The lancing pain in her heart proved the words to be false. At that moment, she craved nothing else but to see Chad walking away from that burning building, safe and sound.

Rocky was still shouting at the police officer and struggling to free himself when Tom appeared and sprinted up to them.

Rocky shot him a desperate look. "Chad's in the attic. Trapped."

Tom didn't hesitate. He raced past the officer and charged through the back office door, heedless of shouted orders from the cop and the firefighters.

Dory's head felt like it would explode. How long did it take to die of smoke inhalation? Terror coursed through her like the water gunning through the fire hose. The firefighters followed the path Tom had taken, spraying water as they went. Seconds turned into minutes. Rocky had gone still now, but his arm where she touched him was tense as strung wire.

"They'll get him out," she said. "They'll save him."

He didn't look at her, just stared into the drifting smoke. Time stood still, and Dory realized she was holding her breath.

"I shouldn't have left him," she whispered to no one. Chad had known he'd never be able to squeeze through the attic window. Maybe if they'd stayed downstairs, worked harder at battering the door…

Her father pulled up in his car, bounded from the driver's side and ran to her. "I heard the sirens and turned around. What happened?"

"Someone trapped us in the storage room and started a fire. I got out through the attic, but Chad couldn't fit.

He's…" She started to cry, tears streaming down her cheeks. He folded her in his arms.

"It's okay. It's going to be okay."

But it wasn't. It couldn't be if Chad died in that smoke. *You're a great mom, Dory. Now go.* He was proud of her and she wanted desperately to tell him how much that meant to her. He could not be gone. It could not be possible.

Her father tensed. Jerking her head up, she saw Tom emerging from the blackness carrying Chad over his shoulder.

A scream sprang from her lips and she ran to them. Rocky and Pete followed. Tom's face was covered in soot as he set Chad down on the far end of the lot. She knelt next to him, stroking his sooty face. "Chad…" was all she could get out.

His eyes were closed, but he was breathing. "Dear God, thank You that he's alive," she gasped.

"We need help here," her father shouted, and a paramedic hustled over.

"You're going to make it, Chad. Can you hear me?" Dory said. The medic immediately slipped an oxygen mask over Chad's mouth and nose.

Rocky clasped Tom's arm. "You okay?"

Tom coughed and nodded. "Yeah. Fire wasn't too big yet. Lots of smoke. Someone poured kerosene on the carpet and set fire to it. Wedged the door."

Dory tried to control her sobbing. "How did you get it unstuck?"

"I didn't." He grinned and held up a nail. "Fortunately, I had a nail in my pocket from working on the barn. Used it to pop the door off its hinges. Chad was already down in the storage room, so I scooped him up and got out of there."

Dory threw her arms around him and squeezed him tight. "Thank you so much, Tom."

He shifted uncomfortably and she let him go.

"Nothing to it," he said.

She got on her knees again and brushed the debris from Chad's hair, stroking his cheek. "It's gonna be okay," she whispered through her tears. "As soon as you open your eyes."

A medic urged her away while he tended to Chad.

The officer came over and introduced himself. "Did you hear anyone in the building before the fire?"

"No," she said, waving away the paramedic who wanted to check her out. "We were looking at a file and someone pulled the door closed and shoved something under the door, but we didn't see who it was."

"Motive?"

Pete grunted. "Whoever didn't want you two looking into my file."

"Blaze," Tom said through gritted teeth.

The cop frowned. "Why would he set a fire? Most people have their information backed up on computers, so he wouldn't be destroying anything that can't be accessed another way, right?"

"That's right. Police have copies of our notes," her father said sheepishly, "even if I haven't gotten around to scanning them all into the computer."

Dory knew from Tom's face that he shared her thought. The fire might not have been about destroying evidence.

"Blaze doesn't want anyone messing up his plans," Tom said. "He works through intimidation."

Dory recalled his getting the picture of Ivy. "True," she said. "He wants to scare us off looking into the boat accident again."

Tom shoved his hands into his pockets. "It's working. Angela is plenty scared. She called Pete to help her look through the evidence. If Blaze did plot the sinking…"

The cop had paused his pencil. "Hold on a minute. I'm gonna need to be brought up to speed here."

Dory briefly explained while the officer's eyes grew wider. He dutifully wrote down the details and promised to relay the information to Danny Patron.

Dory stayed by Chad's side, as did Rocky, as Chad was loaded into the ambulance to be transported to the hospital. Seeing him lying there, still and quiet, was so unnatural. She fought hard against a new wave of tears.

Tom shook his head. "Came over figuring I was going to keep Rocky out of trouble. Didn't figure on a burning building. Keep me updated about Chad, will you? I'll go inform Gus and Ginny. Better to tell them in person, I think, instead of a phone call."

"Of course we will." Dory didn't try to hug him again, but she clasped his calloused hand. "Thank you, Tom."

He climbed into the ranch truck.

"I'll drive you to the hospital," her father said, "and you're going to get checked out while you're there."

She nodded, burning with eagerness to get to Chad.

Her father chewed his lip as they drove, a sure tell that he was twisting the matter over in his mind just like she was.

"Let's try to keep things factual. The arsonist could have been following you—that's the most obvious conclusion—and saw an opportunity to scare you."

"Or the arsonist knew about the files and figured we'd be coming here sooner or later, and watched for an opportunity. You were assisting the DA in the case. That's a matter of public record. Anyone could look it up."

He inclined his head. "Humor me. Who was involved back then who's in the picture now, too? And who could have known you were on your way here?"

She counted off the names of all the people who came to mind. "Any cops and reporters who were involved, of course. The ranch hands and Chad's adopted family. And Blaze, Rocky, Tom, Angela."

He thought it over. "Seems like we can expunge Tom from the list since he just put his life at risk to save Chad. So that leaves Blaze and Angela. Their stories contradict each other. One of them, or both of them, is lying."

Both of them. That was an angle that hadn't occurred to her. "Could they possibly be working together?" She put the scenario together. "They plotted to kill Mary so the inheritance would all go to Angela and she would give him a cut of the bigger pie, not just his trust fund payout. Surely that's far-fetched. They both loved Mary, didn't they?"

Pete sighed. "Dory, I've seen people do terrible things for money. It wouldn't be the first time someone murdered a family member out of greed."

Her head throbbed and she leaned back against the seat. What had she started by reopening the Blaze Turner case? Would any more lives be sacrificed before the truth was out?

She closed her eyes against the memory of Chad motionless in that stretcher.

The case had to be closed before it got any worse.

* * *

Chad was awakened by unfamiliar voices, soft clangs and beeps. He strained to hear the horses whinnying, Meatball and Jingles barking their joyful greeting. Gradually he ascertained that he was in the hospital. Worse yet, he was wearing a ridiculous green gown with an oxygen mask over his face. The fire. He pulled off the mask and sat up so quickly his head spun. "Dory?"

"Right here."

Her hair was wet from a recent shower and she was wearing clean clothes, but when she bent so he could see her, he got a whiff of smoke. Or maybe it was coming from him. Didn't matter. She was unhurt, as far as he could see. He let out a deep breath that made his lungs ache. "You hurt?"

"No, thanks to you." She pressed a kiss to his cheek that temporarily made him forget his thundering headache.

"How'd I get out?"

She smiled, showing that delicate cheek dimple. "I'd like to report that you battered the door down and manfully charged through the flames, but actually, Tom Rourke went in and popped off the door hinges and carried you out. You'd already climbed back down to the storage room before you passed out."

He groaned. "I owe him one."

"I do, too."

He blinked at her.

Her cheeks turned pink. "He saved Ivy's daddy. I'll always owe him for that."

Ivy's daddy. He let that roll around in his soul. He was somebody's daddy. The responsibility of it made him quiver inside.

Her eyes darkened and the cheeky grin disappeared. "Chad, I shouldn't have said we don't need you. It's not true."

His heart beat faster as she leaned close. He wished she would touch his face, kiss him again. The craving to be connected to her in some way floored him. When she was close, it felt as though they were meant to be that way. Together.

"Ivy needs you in her life."

His heart rate slowed. *Ivy, but not you.* He felt an odd mixture of pleasure and pain that made him wonder what he had wished her to say. That she wanted him back? *Not gonna happen. Life isn't a fairy tale.* A coughing spell saved him from having to wrangle any more conversation.

Dory handed him a cup of water and guided the straw to his lips. "She's waiting downstairs to see you, by the way. Grandma brought her."

"Ivy? Here?" His stomach flipped. "I don't want her to see me wearing this getup."

"That is a standard-issue hospital gown." She tucked her hair behind her ear. "I could offer to iron it for you."

It was a long-standing joke between them. Dory was clueless about ironing, yet she'd offered to press his best shirt for a church Christmas party the year after they'd graduated high school. Distracted by a phone call, she'd burned a hole clear through the front. He'd gone to the party in a borrowed shirt instead.

At least it doesn't have wrinkles, he'd said before she'd burst into hysterical tears.

Chad drank more water. "You would really tease a guy who was nearly cooked like a rotisserie chicken?"

"Absolutely."

He chuckled. "That's the Dory I know and love." As the last word left his mouth, his skin went clammy. "I just meant…"

"I know." She went to the window and fussed with the blinds. "The doctor said you might be able to go home this afternoon."

"No 'might' about it. I'm going home. I want to hear exactly what Danny Patron knows about Blaze's whereabouts. And further…" He'd just flipped the covers back when Sarah knocked on the door.

"Someone's here to see you, Mr. Jaggert." She guided Ivy in.

Like a shot, Chad was back under the covers. Ivy stood there in a pink dress, her hair done up in pigtails. Each pigtail had a colored elastic holding it in place. She was as fresh and perfect as a spring blossom.

And here he was, stinking of smoke, a day's worth of stubble on his chin, without even a stitch of his own clothing on. Some father figure. He struggled to sit up as Dory kissed Ivy and lifted her onto one hip.

The girl solemnly surveyed the hospital room, and with a lurch he realized she shared his way of taking it all in, getting the lay of the land, before she spoke. Like father, like daughter. He nearly gaped at the flat-out wonder of it.

He had to clear his throat twice before his voice started working. "Hello, Ivy. I, uh… Thanks for coming to see me. I'm going home soon. Any minute now, actually."

She nodded and handed him a clay pot that held a tender green shoot. "It's gonna be a pumpkin. You could grow it on your ranch with the other ones."

He blinked and accepted the pot, examining it carefully. "Well, that's a fine thing. I haven't had time to plant much this year. I'm sure Aunt Ginny would let me settle it in the garden."

"Her."

"Huh?"

"The plant is a girl. Her name is Polly."

After a long moment, he recovered. "Oh, right. Polly the Pumpkin."

"Can I come and see Meatball? Mommy says he's a real funny puppy."

The ranch? Could she? He was suddenly engulfed with a burning desire to show his daughter all the wondrous things that he loved most deeply at the Roughwater. Waves that kissed the shore. Cliffs that divided green grassland from the beach. The way the sun turned the land from gold to green and signaled the wildflowers to open their fancy faces.

"You are welcome there anytime," he said. "Lots to see. Horses and cattle and dogs." For the first time in his life, he was babbling. He made a mental note to quit already when her next sentence floored them both.

"Can I call you Daddy?"

"What?" He and Dory spoke at the same time. His eyes, he was sure, were bulging out of their sockets.

"Why do you ask, honey?" Dory said in a voice so calm she could have been discussing dinner plans.

"I heard Grandma tell Grandpa that Mr. Chad was my daddy." The girl's gaze lingered on Chad and he had no idea what he was supposed to say. Dory settled a glance on him that seemed to put everything in order. *There will be no more deception*, he read in her expression. Dory did not need him as a partner, but his child did. It would be enough.

Dory smiled at him. "What do you think, Mr. Chad?"

Swallowing the lump in his ravaged throat, he looked at his daughter. "Yes, Ivy. I would be pleased if you would like to call me Daddy."

FIFTEEN

Dory shored up her resolve as she drove Chad back to the ranch shortly after two to gather her belongings from the saddlery. Things were moving altogether too fast. Ivy now knew Chad was her father, and Dory had been pressured into agreeing that Ivy would visit the ranch. Her daughter's reaction was a foregone conclusion. She would fall deeply in love with the place and the people as soon as she set one tiny foot on the Roughwater. And then what would happen to their plans to move to Arizona? The new school she'd chosen so carefully, the small apartment near her mother and father's place?

Though part of Dory was happy, thrilled that Chad and Rocky would be a part of Ivy's life, she wasn't prepared for the tidal wave that threatened with having Chad around on a permanent basis. He unsettled her, threw her off balance, and she'd worked too hard to let anything chip away at her confidence.

He wants to be close because of Ivy. That's all. What's wrong with that?

Nothing. God wanted families to be together. So why the fluttering cascade of tension in her stomach? It was time for some good old-fashioned common sense. Best to work the case from her home base, help her father recover salvageable files from the burned office and follow the plans she'd made for their future in Arizona. She could keep a close eye out for Blaze or Angela or whoever else was involved, and distance herself from the confusing emotional morass until she figured out how to integrate a long-distance father into Ivy's life.

She was working up the courage to tell Chad about her decision as they pulled up the ranch drive, but he had his own agenda.

"I'm going to check on the horses. I'll find you in the saddlery after. We can try to dig up your father's digital files on the case and put our heads together about what we remember."

"But, Chad..."

He was already out of the truck. He'd made it two steps when he froze and raced back, reaching into the front seat for the plant.

"Almost forgot Polly." His grin was equal parts chagrin and wonder.

And that was it. Everything went quivery inside her. That grin, that smile, that softness, melted her heart like the countless marshmallows they'd toasted over campfires on the beach. Chad Jaggert, the boy she'd fallen for madly as a teen, was now a man who still owned her heart. She ached to embrace him, to span his wide shoulders with her arms and press her face into the familiar hollow of his neck. She did not know how it was possible, after he'd discarded her and they'd started up new lives. Maybe her heart would always be linked to his, though hers beat with tenderness and his was fueled by duty and responsibility. Try as she might, she could not deny Chad's power over her…but she could still escape it.

"I'm going back home, Chad…" she blurted, but he was already too far away to hear. Exasperated, she threw the truck into Park and tried to catch up with his long-legged strides. Plant pot clutched under his arm, he marched directly to the paddock. Tom, Liam and Mitch looked up from their conversation. Jingles barked and Meatball raced immediately to Dory, pawing at her knee. She bent to scratch the velvet spot behind his ears.

"I see you're living up to the family reputation of completely ignoring all doctor's advice," Liam said. "Hello, Dory."

She smiled and hoisted Meatball in her arms. "As a matter of fact, the doctor did suggest Chad lie down and take it easy."

Chad waved an irritated hand. "I'm fine. Wanted to check on Boss."

Mitch jerked a thumb at the horse standing next to Zephyr, tail swishing.

"He's in better shape than you are."

Chad didn't seem to hear. "Been thinking he's such a poor drinker. Sweats heavily. Gonna give him an electrolyte supplement."

Tom nodded. "That's what I figured, too. I already told Liam."

"And I took care of it," Liam said. He pointed to Chad's potted plant. "You thought maybe some fresh greens might help old Boss?"

Chad stared at the pot in his hands as if wondering how the thing had gotten into his possession. "It's, uh, a present. From, er…" She saw his shoulders lift as if he'd just sucked in a deep breath. "My daughter." He jerked a tentative look at Dory. "Our daughter. Her name's Ivy. She's almost five."

All three men stared, and heat crawled up Dory's neck. Meatball slathered a tongue along the side of her cheek.

Mitch was the first to react. "Congratulations to both of you. Jane will want to arrange playdates immediately for Charlie and Ivy, I expect. We got a nice little pony she can ride."

Playdates. Pumpkin plants. Ponies. *Panic.* Meatball wriggled to let Dory know she was holding him too snugly. She set him on the ground. "That might be nice sometime. She's very busy with school and such." *And we're moving out of state*, she decided not to say aloud.

"Well, that's just grand." A grin engulfed Liam's face. "And your first dad assignment is to plant Polly Pumpkin?"

Chad gaped. "How did you…?"

Dory turned the pot around so Chad could see that Ivy had lettered *Polly* in pink glitter paint on the side. There was even a stick-on jewel in the center of the *o*.

Flushed scarlet, Chad gripped the pot, ignored his brother and turned to Tom. "Didn't thank you properly for getting me out of the fire."

Tom shrugged. "Nothing you wouldn't have done for me. I thought I was going to be keeping Rocky out of harm's way. Did the cops catch sight of Blaze at the fire?"

Dory shook her head. "Not yet. They're interviewing potential witnesses. Tom, how long have you known Angela?"

He rubbed a hand over his stubbled chin. "She looked me up when Mary wanted to buy a horse for Blaze on his sixteenth birthday." His mouth quirked in a faint smile. "Angela put me through the wringer making sure they weren't getting ripped off. I've helped out with her horses since then."

"Did you know Angela had arranged a meeting with Dory's father just before the fire?" Chad said.

Tom's mouth tightened. "What are you getting at?"

Dory tried for a soothing tone. "We're looking into all the angles."

Tom shrugged. "I get it, but you're chasing the wrong horse. Angela is trying to protect herself from Blaze since the cops can't seem to catch him. She's a good woman, and she's been through a lot. Her sister was her best friend."

Mary...the woman whose death was firmly on Rocky's shoulders. Dory suppressed a shiver. "Do you think it's possible that the sinking all those years ago wasn't an accident?"

"I don't see how it could have been intentional." Puzzlement played over his weathered face. "Wait a minute. Are you saying you think Angela might be involved in that?"

Chad shrugged. "Just floating ideas."

"Well, you can hobble that one. My mom used to say some people are cut from a finer cloth. Angela is like that. She would never hurt her sister or anyone else. Find Blaze. He's the one you should be looking for." Tom was clearly done with the conversation.

Something about the way he'd said it.

...cut from a finer cloth.

It became clear to Dory in that moment. *Tom, I know your secret.*

"I'll get the feed loaded up." He jammed a pair of leather gloves into his back pocket and strode away.

Dory realized the three brothers were looking at her, probably wondering at the calculating look on her face.

"You got an idea, Dory?" Liam asked.

Not an idea. Not exactly. Something inside told her it was a fact. "I think Tom is in love with Angela Robertson."

Chad gaped. "What? How do you know that?"

"Call it a woman's intuition."

Mitch laughed. "Same way Aunt Ginny knew when Liam wrecked the truck and didn't want to come clean about it."

Liam whistled. "Gotta say, I didn't see that one coming. Tom's not exactly a lady killer. He's been out on a few dates, but nothing's stuck. I guess a highbrow damsel can fall for a simple cowboy. Jane and Maggie did it."

"I'm not sure the feeling is mutual for Tom and Angela." She caught Chad's eye. "It could be that Tom loves Angela, but she doesn't feel the same."

"Yeah, and maybe she's using him." Liam frowned. "That goes against my grain. Tom's a good man, honest and straightforward."

Chad exhaled long and slow. "If he loves her enough, could be he just doesn't want to see her ugly side."

"Love is blind," Mitch said.

Mitch's dark eyes followed Tom's progress. "And that kind of love can be dangerous."

If Tom Rourke had put his heart in the hands of a killer, it might just be fatal.

* * *

Chad escorted Dory back to the saddlery. Meatball had decided to join them, making his own zigzag path but never straying too far from Dory's side. She was quiet and tense. He wasn't sure if she was thinking about Tom or any other of the hundreds of strange details swirling around the case, so he fired off a comment.

"Tom's a good guy, and he's plenty strong. If it turns out Angela is a killer, he'll survive it. I'll go borrow a laptop from the ranch house and you can see if your dad's files are intact somewhere in cyberspace."

She paused on the saddlery porch. "I'm going home, Chad."

Going home. She actually intended to leave right then? "But…we haven't gotten answers to anything. I thought my father's case was your top priority." It wasn't fair to call her motives into question, but he felt a rising tide of desperation.

She hushed him by touching his hand. "It's too much. I've been on my own for five years and now there's uncles and grandparents and…"

"And me."

"Yes, and you." Her gaze was gentle. "I know it was my own choice to go it alone, but now I've got to figure out how to make this all work, and there are multiple families involved."

The desperation rose higher. "Don't take her away from me." He recognized the pleading in his tone.

Her mouth wobbled, and now her fingers found his face, cupping his cheek, silky soft. "Chad, you're Ivy's father. I will make sure you know her and she knows you. There will be plenty of time for that whether I'm here or in Rock Ridge or Arizona."

"No, there won't. Especially if you move to Arizona."

"When…not if."

"All the more reason for you to stick close now. She just learned I'm her daddy."

"I just…need some space to figure out how this will look."

He couldn't help himself. He turned his mouth so his lips grazed her palm. His soul craved her comfort. He allowed his face to rest there and he imagined for a flickering moment that she desired the connection, too.

"God wants you to be a father to Ivy. I understand that now and I won't ever deny you that right again." She paused. "You trusted me a long time ago, Chad," she whispered. "Can you do it again?"

Trust her? Could he even trust himself? He'd treated her so abominably, yet here she was, asking him. He couldn't answer. Instead he pressed a kiss to her wrist.

She pulled away.

The rejection was unmistakable. Of course. The issue under discussion was parenting, not anything more. *Chad, what is your problem? You and Dory are almost friends again. Can't you let well enough alone? You're parents. That's it.*

He scrambled for a way to smooth things over. "I understand why you think you need to leave right now, but it isn't safe for you to be off on your own investigating Blaze and Angela."

Now her hands found her hips and the mettle showed. "It's my job. I've been doing it for years. I have my dad, and besides, we've been half drowned here in Driftwood and almost incinerated back home, so both places call for caution."

He wished he could think of something, anything, to keep her there on the ranch, but he could not dredge up a single compelling argument. "I'll drive you back," he conceded. "But can we talk to Aunt Ginny and arrange a ranch visit for Ivy first? Please?"

The teenage Chad would never have been able to present his deepest desire calmly, with a "please" tacked on at the end, no less. And yet he had, and in his own ears it came out the way a rational, mature, grown-up-father-type person would sound. It astonished him. Aunt Ginny always said God used messes for masterpieces. Maybe she was on to something. The teen Dory might have made a joke or bowled him over with her emotional reaction to a disagreement. He waited.

She considered, tugging at a strand of her white-blond hair. "Okay. That's fair."

Mentally he high-fived himself. So there was such a thing as compromise in parenting, in trust that transcended personal desire. It was something his mom hadn't shown him, but his confidence in Dory's mothering rose even higher, as did his fragile faltering belief in himself. He nodded. "Thank you."

She smiled. That sweet smile that showed the dimple again. There was something reserved in it, though, a formality that preserved some distance between them. The few feet between them stretched into miles he could not cross even on his fastest horse.

"You're welcome."

"All right," he said with a sigh. "I guess it's time to drop the bombshell on Aunt Ginny and Uncle Gus."

They walked to the main house. Meatball meandered

along with them. They found Gus and Ginny sorting through invoices in the living room. As much as Chad tried to downplay the revelation of his sudden fatherhood, the announcement seemed to set them both into near giddiness.

"Of course Ivy can visit. How about Tuesday?" Ginny beamed. "I'm so excited to meet her." She accepted the potted pumpkin reverently, as if it were a precious newborn. "I've got the perfect spot for Polly the Pumpkin. The pole beans are ready for the second planting and maybe she'd like to help put in the tomatoes."

Gus winked. "Oh, you've got Aunt Ginny off and running now that she knows Ivy's a gardener. Guess you'll have the horse introductions covered."

"Figured I'd let her help with the currying in case she's a bit fearful at first. I…" Chad sneaked a look at Dory. Was he being too pushy? Assuming too much? Asserting himself as a dad before he had a right to?

Dory chewed her lip, which he took as a sign to ease up on the reins. "Over time, I mean. Not all at once, of course. Whatever Dory thinks is best."

Her pleased expression told him he'd done it right, and he made a mental note to follow her lead where Ivy was concerned until he got the knack of things and Ivy felt more comfortable.

Chad's phone rang with a call from Mitch. He put it on speaker.

"I just phoned Danny to get an update. He asked me to share an interesting bit of information he unearthed. Turns out Angela's father was a competitive marksman."

Chad cocked his head. "Is that right?"

"Angela took up his passion for shooting. Won a

couple of awards and such back in the day as a father/daughter rifle team."

Chad locked eyes with Dory. Angela Robertson was skilled with a rifle. Was she the one who'd taken a shot at them at the gorge? He sucked in a breath, ravaged lungs burning.

Was Angela a woman "cut from a finer cloth"? Or a calculated killer?

The list of potential victims scrolled in his mind. What if Dory's investigations made her the victim of another attack? Now she was determined to return home, where he could not keep her safe. His muscles locked up tight as if his body sensed a fuse burning away the final seconds before an explosion.

He had to find out the truth.

Lives hung in the balance.

Lives that were beyond precious.

His wife and daughter.

SIXTEEN

Dory's escape plans were put on hold when Chad was called to assist with a cow that had become ensnared by the limbs of a fallen tree. The animal was panicked, and the extraction would be both dangerous and delicate.

"It's gonna take all hands for this one. I'll be back soon as I can."

She'd watched him ride off on Zephyr, tall and easy in the saddle. The late-afternoon hour lent some urgency to the endeavor. Wrestling a cow in the dark would be nearly impossible. She finished packing and spent some time online looking for tidbits about Blaze. Nothing new came to her attention. For a change of pace, she took Meatball outside and engaged in an impromptu dog-training session.

"Sit, Meatball." The dog focused his black button eyes on her intently, then rolled directly onto his back, three legs waving and his tummy offered up for scratches. She laughed and tried again. After the fifth attempt, she sank to the ground in her own "sit" and snuggled with the silly pup. "We're gonna have to work on that. Maybe Ivy can convince you to sit."

An image of Ivy and the exuberant Meatball rose

in her mind. Ivy resisted her better attempts at training sometimes, too. At the moment, she could not be induced to clean up her room except under threat of dire consequences. Plus the child was a pack rat to the core. Ivy and Meatball would be partners in crime, she decided. Meatball was yet another reason Ivy would likely never want to leave the ranch. The tug of a new life in Arizona compelled her. Wouldn't it all be so much easier if they had a little distance from Chad? Yes, she thought. Distance would allow her to think things through. Still, the muscles deep down in her stomach remained knotted.

The temperature dropped as a bank of pewter clouds rolled in from the ocean. Wind tickled her skin into gooseflesh. The smell of rain hung heavy in the air. "Come on, Meatball. Looks like it's going to storm." Dory went back inside for a windbreaker and a few sips of water to soothe her smoke-damaged throat.

She picked up her phone, and her screen showed two missed calls, from a number she didn't recognize, along with a message. She played the voice mail.

"Dory, it's Rocky. I hope you're feelin' okay. Just wanted to ask you a question about Blaze. I thought I spotted him, but I need a better description. I haven't seen him since…" He trailed off.

Since he'd supposedly died on Rocky's boat.

"Your dad promised we could chat, but he isn't answering his phone. I figure he's busy cleaning up the mess at his office. Chad's not answering, either. Anyway, call me when you get this message. Oh, and I'm mighty proud to find out I'm a grandpa."

Her nerves jangled. He'd seen Blaze? The calls had come in just a few minutes apart. Quickly she redialed.

"Pick up, Rocky. Pick up." The phone rang and rang with no answer except a computerized message informing her that Rocky had not set up his voice mail. He was not one to fool with technology, she recalled.

Pulse skittering, she remembered, too, that he was also not one to wait around for a return call. What if he'd gone after Blaze on his own? He was determined before the office fire to apologize to Blaze for what had happened to his mother. After Chad was almost killed, Rocky might have had a change of view and decided to force a confrontation for another reason. Either way, she had to get to him before he put himself at risk.

There was no sign of Chad's return, so she texted him. Meet me at Rocky's.

Meatball yipped as she grabbed her keys. She jogged to the car, thankful for the newly repaired window that kept out the spitting rain. Meatball torpedoed into the passenger seat as soon as she pulled the door open.

"All right, but you're going to stay out of trouble, right?" She didn't think Meatball's listening skills were any better than his ability to sit on command. Nonetheless, she found the young dog's company a comfort. He peered at her, three legs tucked neatly underneath him, and she could almost detect a smile on that doggy face. She wished she felt as cheerful about their adventure.

Chad had told her that Rocky lived in a trailer near the dock since his release from prison. Formerly it had functioned as an office, a base of operations for his fishing excursion business. She took the rough road up to the grassy field where the trailer was positioned. Did it pain Rocky to be able to look down at the crawling ocean and watch others ply their boats for profit when he was no longer permitted to do so? She did not know if the stripping of his captain's license was permanent. Perhaps he would never trust himself again to be responsible for passengers after what had happened.

Fingers tight on the steering wheel, she guided the car to a spot next to a beat-up station wagon.

Meatball hopped down next to her when she got out and immediately meandered to the tall grasses to sniff. She figured Rocky wouldn't mind a canine visitor. The winding path to Rocky's front door was dotted with clay pots containing succulents of all description. Dory smiled. Maybe the green thumb really did run in the family.

The front porch was home to a rocking chair, the blue cushion darkening with spots as the rain grew heavier. The aroma of garlic and onions from inside made her mouth water. It brought her back to high school, when Rocky would make his self-declared world-famous omelets for Chad and Dory. They'd eaten at a wobbly table with mismatched forks, the complete opposite of the neat dinner presentations offered by her mother at their formal dining table. She thought she'd never enjoyed meals quite as much as those sloppy omelets served precariously on cheap paper plates.

She'd raised a knuckle to knock when Meatball started to bark. She whirled around. The scruff on the back of Meatball's neck was raised, every muscle in his compact body stiff with tension. His high-pitched bark sounded over the pattering rain. She strained to see, wiping the raindrops from her cheeks.

She couldn't make out anything moving in the trees that edged the property. She clutched her phone, ready to dial the police. Or should she call Chad? He probably wouldn't even hear his phone.

A ground squirrel streaked past so close he almost trod on her toes. She squealed and jumped back as Meatball bulleted past her and disappeared into the wet greenery. Relief swamped her nerves along with the irritation. *Just a squirrel.* Heart thumping, she went after the dog.

"Meatball," she hollered at the edge of the trees. "Come back here right now."

The rain began to fall in earnest as she called again. When he didn't reappear, she whistled. Still no dog. Any other time she wouldn't have hesitated to jog right into the trees and round up the runaway animal. Any other time…when memories of plummeting to the bottom of the chasm or being smothered in a blanket of smoke weren't quite so fresh. When a person had recently been a target, strolling off alone in a strange area was off the agenda. Smart to be cautious. Chad would be proud of her.

She decided to return to Rocky's trailer to ask for his help. A strange feeling caused the hairs at the base of her neck to prickle. *Someone's here.*

She spun around, her heart slamming against her ribs.

Blaze was standing not five feet away, hands in his pockets, head cocked as if hearing a far-off noise. His damp hood clung to his head as he stared her down.

"Blaze." The breath froze in her lungs. "What are you doing here?"

He didn't answer, just reached into the pocket of his sweatshirt. His lips twitched in a slight smile.

"Rocky!" she shouted. "Blaze is out here."

There was no answer, no sign of movement from the trailer. If he was cooking, he had probably not heard her scream over the noise and the pelting rain. Her skin crawled as she realized she was all alone with the man who had almost crushed her with a boulder, someone who had used her daughter's picture to manipulate her into meeting with him.

Blaze Turner was a wanted man, a liar, and possibly much worse. Panic immobilized her but she forced herself to make a plan.

Get away. Call for help.

There was no way to get around Blaze to Rocky's trailer and she wasn't sure his door would be unlocked anyway. Blaze was also blocking her route to her car. A hundred feet to her left, she made out a trail winding through the tall grass. It cut through the field, but she was not sure where it led. A trail might mean another trailer site or maybe a ranch home. All she needed was a momentary hiding place, long enough to place a call. There was no more time to think it out.

"It's way past time to finish this." Blaze took a knife from his pocket, flicking open the blade. The moment he took a step forward, she was in motion, running as far and as fast as she could manage.

Over the sound of her own frantic movement, she heard his pursuit. Dory's nerves pulsed with fear as she sprinted down the path. Ahead was a bent iron gate that had once barred the road. The padlock was long gone and the gate shoved aside. She hardly slowed, pushing past. Jerking a look back terrified her. Blaze was close. His fingers reached out and grabbed at the fabric of her jacket.

With a cry, she surged forward.

I won't let you catch me.

He lunged at her again and this time he got a fistful

of her hood. The jacket pulled taut across her throat and she gagged. Combined fear and fury propelled her just enough that she yanked free of his grip, but her momentum carried her over onto one knee. She felt the thin jean fabric tear away as the rocks scraped at her skin. Scrambling upright, she ran on.

Her senses were dulled by panic.

"Stop running," Blaze shouted behind her.

Stop, so you can kill me? Her legs churned faster, widening the distance between them. The trees closed in ahead. There she would find a hiding place.

Without warning, the ground gave way beneath her. A slab of dirt seemed to break loose. She was caught in a cloud of choking debris. The bottom dropped out of her stomach as she fell some ten feet until she landed back-first on the ground. The breath was slammed from her lungs.

When the sparks cleared, she found herself staring up into the storm-washed sky that seemed impossibly far away. What had happened?

Blinking hard, she sought to bring her senses back on track.

After a half dozen slow breaths, Dory sat up. Her lungs were working, and a cautious test proved her limbs were still functional. *Blaze*, her brain screamed. He hadn't been that far behind. She leaped to her feet, sinking ankle-deep into a wet layer of leaves. Pulling herself free, she slogged to what she'd thought must be a wall of earth. Instead she found a curved section of rusted metal.

The truth dawned on her slowly. She'd fallen into some sort of decrepit cistern. The thing hadn't been used in decades, most likely. The iron fence had been intended to keep people out. The cistern was a good twelve feet across, littered with a layer of debris. Though she skimmed her palms over the walls, she could find no ladder or steps leading up and out. Fighting tears, she moved faster and faster around the periphery. There was no escape. She was trapped like a snared animal. Her body went cold.

"Don't panic," she told herself. Maybe Blaze hadn't seen her fall. She'd wait silently; send a text to Chad or the police department. They'd get her out.

Willing her brain not to entertain any other possibilities, she pulled out her phone. *Please let there be a signal. Please.* There wasn't. *Move to a different spot. Try again.*

She'd crept only a few steps when she sensed his presence.

Neck craning upward, she saw Blaze smiling down at her.

"Stuck, huh?"

"They…" She swallowed. "They know I'm here."

"No one knows you're here," he said. "It's just you and me now."

She swallowed hard. "I'm no threat to you."

"Right. How much is my aunt paying you to come after me?"

"I'm not working for Angela."

The whites of his eyes gleamed. "You lie. That's why you tracked me here to the canyon. She was going to meet with your father at his office, wasn't she?"

"How do you know that?"

He shrugged. "None of your business."

"Is that why you set the fire?"

"I didn't set any fire."

She threw his words back at him. "Now you're lying."

She did not catch his reply over the moan of the wind. "Why did you come back to Driftwood, Blaze?"

"To get my money." His tone was sullen. "My mother wanted me to have it. It's mine. Decided to quit running and take what's due me before Auntie Dearest had me declared legally dead."

"Fine, then." Dory fired off a challenge. "Man up and go to the police. Tell them who you are and claim your inheritance. Why are you hiding out? Afraid you'll be arrested for the ATM robbery?"

"That was a mistake. I didn't have anything to do with that. Wrong place. Wrong time. Story of my life."

Playing the victim? she thought. Instead she said, "Okay, then you haven't done anything wrong. Go to the police and you're a rich man."

"I've got to take care of some things first."

The way he said it chilled her. "Like killing your aunt so you get her part of the family money, too?"

His laugh was bitter. "You've got it all backward. She deserves what she gets, and you deserve it, too, for helping her."

"I didn't—"

A streak of lightning sizzled across the sky followed by a rumble of thunder.

"Enough of this." His tone softened. "Come here where I can reach you. I'll find a branch and lower it down to help you out. We can talk."

"No way."

"I'm tired of running and hiding out, half starved and freezing all the time. Staying in this town is worse than sleeping in the subway. I want this over and you're going to help me end it."

"I'm not helping you, Blaze." She retreated until her back was against the cold cistern wall, as far away from him as she could get.

Terrified as she was, she knew he would be a fool to jump down into the cistern with her and trap himself. They were at an impasse. All she had to do was to wait him out. She frantically tapped out a text to Chad.

Her phone flashed out the message No Service.

Not surprising since she was trapped in a big metal coffin. She pressed Send anyway.

Just stay calm. He can't hurt you from up there. Her prison might be her salvation.

A moment later, she realized just how wrong she'd been when something sailed down from above and struck her on the shoulder before ricocheting off the metal wall with the sound of a struck bell.

Pain sparked white-hot. She cried out. Scrambling for the thing that had bounced off her shoulder, Dory snatched it up, intending to hurl it back up at him. It was a useless thought. Instead she jammed it into her pocket, scrambled for her phone to try another text from a slightly different location. Still no signal. Her breathing was ragged with panic. A familiar bark sounded loud and Meatball poked his head over the edge, darting away when Blaze threw a rock at him.

"Don't you hurt my dog," Dory shrieked.

"Reminds me of my dog. Dear Auntie Angela left the gate open one night and I never saw him again." He lobbed another rock. Meatball squealed and ran off into the night. Blaze returned his attention to her, hurling another rock into the cistern that struck a stinging blow on her hip.

"I'm a really good shot. I had a lot of time to practice

since I got cut from the baseball team." He threw a second rock that missed her head by inches. It struck the metal with an echoing clang. "I've got nowhere to go."

And Dory had nowhere to hide as he hurled the next rock straight at her.

When they'd finally freed the bawling cow and assessed the wound on her rear leg, Chad checked his messages. He immediately called Dory. No answer. His next call went to his father.

"Is Dory there?"

"Here? Nah. I left a couple of messages for her but she hasn't come."

A strange foreboding swirled in his gut as he left Mitch, Liam and Tom to tend to the cow. "Going to find Dory. She said she went to Dad's, but she isn't there."

"We'll check in with you when we're clear," Liam said, struggling with Mitch to restrain the cow while Tom applied the ointment.

Chad eased into the saddle, water streaming off his cowboy hat. The storm sounds almost drowned out his phone. It was his father again. "Dory's car's next to mine. I can hear a dog barking, but I see no sign of her. I'm going to look."

Her car...no sign of her. He swallowed. "No, Dad. Stay there in case she turns up. I'm on my way."

He guided Zephyr onto a path that would take him right onto Rocky's rented property. He let the horse go as fast as he felt was safe along the rain-soaked grass. It was an easy fifteen-minute ride but he made it in ten. He found his father in a rain slicker and boots at the end of the drive, trying to coax a sodden Meatball to come to him.

Rocky wiped the water off his face. "Dog just barks but he won't come."

Chad slid off Zephyr. "Dory never would have left him alone. Something's happened."

Rocky nodded. "I searched the woods, but there's no sign of her. Only this critter."

Meatball whined and ran a half dozen steps, then turned back and returned to Chad before he repeated the whole operation.

"I'll follow the dog. Call Mitch and Liam." Chad leaped astride Zephyr again. "Go find her, Meatball."

Please find her.

SEVENTEEN

Chad didn't think Meatball had any tracking skills whatsoever, but the dog's body language was unmistakable. Every few yards he would stop and wait for Chad's horse to close the distance, and then he'd be off again. He handled the terrain as easily as if he'd had all four legs to work with.

They drew deeper into the woods. Zephyr picked his way easily over fallen logs and Chad guided him as best he could across the slippery ground until they came to a gate intended to block the road. It was open. The glimmer of his cell phone light revealed a water-filled imprint of a shoe. A small one. Dory-size. There was another imprint, much bigger, clearly belonging to a man.

His pulse roared. "Come on, Meatball. Where is she?"

Meatball whined and surged ahead.

Chad pressed on, willing the little dog to lead the way. When the branches became too low to accommodate horse and rider, Chad slid off, grabbed his rifle, shoved a flashlight into his back pocket and shadowed the dog on foot. Ahead he heard a metallic sound, a cry of pain. The dog burst into motion and Chad did, too, slipping and stumbling.

Was that movement ahead? He did not slow until he arrived in a small clearing in time to see a hooded figure, arm raised as if he was hurling a fastball. Chad snapped the rifle to his shoulder and shouted, "Put it down, right now."

The man changed course and let loose the rock. It glanced off of Chad's elbow enough to spoil his shot. By the time he took aim, the assailant was disappearing into the trees. Everything in him wanted to run Blaze to ground, but Meatball was fixated on something, barking and whining for all he was worth.

Teeth gritted, Chad ran to the dog, almost falling into some sort of void. A cistern, he realized as he skidded to a stop at the rim. Down below, he couldn't make out anything. He shone his flashlight into the darkness. Still he saw nothing, but Meatball was nearing hysterics. He played the light more slowly over the debris littering the bottom. He saw her.

Dory was crouched on her knees, her head in her hands, rolled into a tight ball.

"Dory," he cried, fear sparking across his nerves. "Are you hurt?"

She did not answer, but when he called a second time, she looked up and he saw that her forehead was bloody. Her expression was contorted in pain or fear, he wasn't sure which. Immediately he flattened himself on his stomach as if he could somehow reach her. "Honey, I'm right here. I'm going to get you out, okay? Can you hear me?"

He heard her sob and the sound cut through him like a chain saw through a brittle branch. At that moment, he would have ripped out his own heart if it would have eased her pain.

Meatball got underfoot as he scrambled to his feet and whistled for Zephyr.

The horse ambled out of the trees and Chad fetched a rope from the saddlebag. Mitch and Rocky arrived as he was looping it around his waist.

"What—" Rocky started, but Chad cut him off.

"Dory's down there and she's hurt. Lower me."

In one fluid motion, Mitch looped the rope around a tree. He and Rocky gripped it tightly as Chad slithered over the edge. He hoped he would not cause any debris to rain down on her. He could not close the distance quickly enough. As soon as his boots hit the ground, he shirked off the rope and went to her.

She tumbled into his arms, sobbing and shaking.

"I'm here now," Chad said, trying to calm his own roaring emotions. "I'm going to take care of you."

All around her were rocks of every size, missiles Blaze must have thrown at her. As he realized what Blaze had done, the anger almost choked him. He struggled to breathe. *You have to keep it together for Dory.*

He skimmed her back with his palms. She was wet and he prayed it was with rain, not blood. "We're going to get you out, okay? I've got a rope. Mitch and Rocky will pull us out. You just need to hold on tight. Can you do that? Hold on to me?"

She sucked in another shaky breath and nodded miserably.

He pulled the rope around him again and tightened it, calling up to Mitch and his father. "I've got her. Pull us up slow."

"Copy that," Mitch said, disappearing back into the darkness.

Chad put his arms out and Dory embraced him. Her legs were shaking so badly she could not stand, so he hoisted her. She clasped her ice-cold hands around his neck.

"Ready," he called.

As the rope strained upward, he cradled her. Her body felt so small, her skin frigid. The potent combination of anger and fear left him dizzy. Blaze had hurt Dory. He would pay. Blaze would be punished for what he'd done to her.

He braced his boot heels to absorb the impact against the metal. It was a matter of minutes before they were clear of the rim. His father helped untie the rope. Meatball danced in ecstatic circles, yipping in his desire to get to Dory.

"Bring her back to my trailer. We can call an ambulance from there."

"I don't want to go to the hospital," Dory said.

"But you're—" Chad began to protest.

"I'm not going." There was an edge of hysteria in her voice. Tears started to flow down her face and her mouth went quivery.

"I'll take her back on Zephyr," Chad said, giving Mitch and his father a glance that meant *we can change her mind when we get her back inside*. Mitch and Rocky helped Dory up into Chad's arms.

She was cradled against him, and he heard her teeth chattering. He unzipped his jacket and wrapped it around her, feeding her his warmth.

"He threw rocks at me," she whispered.

"I…" He tried to bite back the rage. "I am going to

make sure he never touches you again." At that moment, he was filled with the iron-strong certainty that he would never let anyone hurt Dory, in any way, ever. Dory Winslow was his and she would have his protection until the last breath was drawn from his dead body.

His? Not anymore. But it was too much to fight through the forest of irrational feeling at that moment, so he did what came naturally—shut his mouth and rode his horse. Her tears wet his flannel shirt, quiet sobs absorbed by his chest until they reached Rocky's trailer. Mitch took Zephyr along with his mare and secured them under the shelter of the oak trees as Chad guided Dory to the trailer.

Rocky led the way inside. "She's soaked. Don't have any suitable clothes, but I figure some of my things will probably cover her from head to toe. What about a hot shower? Some tea?"

He'd never heard his ex-soldier father sound so frantic or uncertain.

Chad bent to look Dory in the eyes. "Can you sit on a kitchen chair for a minute, honey? So we can see if you're bleeding anywhere?"

She sat and he examined her as best he could for wounds. The cut on her forehead had stopped bleeding. Both her knees were scraped through the rips in her jeans and it seemed her shoulder was bruised. Her body trembled violently.

"Can I…take a shower?" she said in a tiny voice. "I'm so cold."

He knelt next to her. "You know, Dory, it would be best if we went to the hospital right now." He touched her cold fingers when she tensed. "Just for a quick checkup."

"Please," she said. "A shower first."

It was wrong. It would probably mess up any evidence and cause more problems if she had a concussion or something. But that *please* just got all up inside him and knocked the steely determination clean out of him. He sighed. "A shower. Then we'll go."

He took her arm and led her into the tiny bathroom, where he started the water. When it was steaming, he left her with a clean towel his father had provided and a well-worn sweatshirt and sweatpants. "I'm going to stay in the hallway in case you need me. Okay?"

When she didn't answer, he put a finger under her chin and eased her face to his. "Okay?" he repeated.

She nodded.

He heard her step inside and slide the shower door closed. Leaning back against the wall, he could not get the muscles in his stomach to unclench. Those rocks… her fear…his own molten rage. It took him a moment to realize Mitch and Rocky were standing at the other end of the hallway, watching him.

"She okay?" Rocky asked softly. "I feel terrible. I texted her to ask about Blaze 'cause I saw him in town. She must have been coming here to talk to me about it. I just didn't hear her knock. I was cooking and the rain and I had the radio on…"

"Not your fault, Dad. This is all on Blaze, and as soon as I know Dory's okay, I'm going to hunt him down."

Mitch folded his arms. "I understand the feeling. We'll find him, together, and then he gets handed over to Danny."

Chad barked out the words. "He threw rocks at her, Mitch."

His brother's dark eyes met his. "The police," he said quietly.

Vengeance, his gut screamed, but Chad knew Mitch was right. Blaze belonged in prison and it was the job of the police to make that happen.

But Blaze had hurt Dory, and if it took every remaining moment of Chad's life, he would ensure that he paid in full for the pain he'd inflicted on her. The terror. All of it.

Go ahead and run, Blaze.
You'll never get far enough away.

Dory stayed in the shower until the hot water was depleted, but it did not wash away the chill deep inside. The bruises where the rocks had impacted were red and sore, on her shoulder, her hip. The worst was the cut across her forehead, not deep but swollen and ugly.

Why hadn't she gone to Rock Ridge right away? Back to her tiny home, her daughter, her life?

Because Rocky was going to pursue Blaze and she'd had to prevent that if she could. Rocky had already served his time in prison, but the sinking would always be a legacy of shame, one she and her father had helped shape. What was the truth about what happened that day?

The facts were still murky and distorted, but one thing was now as clear as glass in her mind. Blaze was not a misunderstood innocent. He was a cruel, self-absorbed thug. She pictured his smile as he'd coolly begun to stone her. She didn't doubt that he would have continued until she was dead. Her hands began to shake.

And, she reminded herself as she gingerly pulled on the sweatshirt and pants, he was on a mission.

I want this over.

She piled her clothes into a filthy bundle and met Chad in the hall. His eyes burned bright and hard, softening when he saw her in a way that made her stomach jump. If he hadn't come...

She swallowed a sob. He pulled her close and pressed his face to her neck. She fought the urge to collapse there, his damp hair pressed against her chin, the beat of his heart comforting as a lullaby.

After a moment, he took her hand and led her to the front room, where Rocky had the space heater on full. He insisted she sit on the old stuffed rocker, which was obviously Rocky's favored seat. Meatball launched himself directly into her lap. She kissed his caramel ears and laid her head against his damp fur. Rocky and Mitch perched on the wooden kitchen chairs and Chad paced.

She remembered how he would pace the hospital corridors the few times his father had required treatment for alcohol poisoning or drunken accidents. It was not the rambling stroll of a person trying to pass the time, but the contained stalking of a wild animal forced into a cage. There was some of that same ferocity in him now. *I am going to make sure he never touches you again.* His passion scared her. So did his tenderness.

You just need to hold on tight. Can you do that? Hold on to me?

It was so easy to commend herself into his care, his protection. But she determined not to let the tide of feeling carry her away. *You're Ivy's mommy.* It was natural he would be protective and angered at anyone who threatened her. That was not love. It was loyalty. She accepted the steaming mug of chamomile tea from Rocky, determined to find the steel in her spine again.

"How did you find me?"

"Meatball." Chad stared at the dog in her lap. "He led me right to you."

She kissed Meatball again. "That's two times you've rescued me."

Mitch eyed her. "Did Blaze say anything to you?"

"He thinks I'm working for Angela."

Rocky shook his head. "Guy's paranoid."

"He said he didn't set the fire and he has some things to take care of before he claims his inheritance."

"He's not going to claim anything," Chad snapped. "He assaulted you. He's going to prison. End of story."

"I think he intends to kill Angela so he'll inherit a larger pot of money, just like we thought."

"As I said, he's not going to get his hands on one thin dime."

"He would if…" She trailed off.

"If what?"

"If he kills Angela…and me without leaving any evidence behind to incriminate himself." She continued before Chad's face drew any darker. "If we could catch him, it might not help anyway. You didn't see him actually hurt me. There's only my testimony. He wouldn't necessarily be convicted."

"I saw him with a rock in his hand," Chad rasped.

"Did you see his face?"

"No, but…"

"It was dark, storming. He'll say it wasn't him. Make up some story about protecting himself or concoct an alibi."

Rocky frowned. "He'd be a fool to put his word against yours."

She thought of Angela's assessment. *He can make*

anyone believe it's not his fault... Somehow he's always the victim. "I don't think he's completely rational. He feels he's been wronged, that his aunt's been hunting him since Mary drowned. He's tired of hiding out. He's probably not going to run anymore."

Even as she said the words, she knew she was right. He would stay put until he'd killed the people who stood in the way of his inheritance. She hadn't realized she'd been crying until a tear plopped onto the front of her borrowed sweatshirt. Meatball whisked away the second with his tongue.

"He's not going to hurt you again," Chad said, taking her hand.

She gulped, forehead throbbing. It was as if she could still hear the rocks smashing down around her. In spite of Chad's strong grip and the reassuring warmth of Meatball in her lap, Dory felt suddenly cold through and through.

I want this over, he'd said.

And he'd meant every word.

EIGHTEEN

Dory had acquiesced about going to the hospital, and that scared Chad more than the bruises and cuts. She'd never been what could be considered compliant. It was one of the things he'd relished about her. The day she was told the high school gym teacher would flunk her best friend, Jeannie, who was unable to climb the rope due to a crippling fear of heights, Dory refused to climb the rope in a show of support. When all the other girls and two boys took her lead and followed suit, the teacher capitulated. He prayed her indomitable spirit was not dulled by what had happened in the cistern.

She'd been efficiently examined and released with painkillers just before seven thirty. He walked her down to the lobby and out into the courtyard, where the street-light caught the nasty bruise on her forehead. She'd pulled down the sleeves of the shirt he'd brought for her to cover the marks on her arms. Seeing the damage, the pain Blaze had inflicted, nearly drove him to distraction. It was all he could do not to tear off on Zephyr and comb every lonely corner in Driftwood until he tracked Blaze down.

But he would not leave Dory, not like this, when she was strangely quiet.

"Are you hurting, Dory?" She shook her head, but he guided her to a seating area with two chairs and a soft patio light. He knelt next to her and put a hand on her knee. He didn't say anything, just tried to show her with his touch how much he hurt for her.

"I was just…" She stopped, pushed the hair back from her face and tried again. "I was trying to figure out what to say to Ivy."

He blinked. What to say? Then he got it. Her face was bruised and battered. What would Ivy think about that? Would she be scared? The tight band in his gut cinched one more notch. Blaze hadn't just hurt Dory. He was responsible for frightening Ivy. Now the protective fire roared inside so loud he almost didn't catch her next words.

"I try to always tell her the truth, but I'm not sure how to explain what happened."

"Sure. I understand. You could stay at the saddlery for a few days, until the marks fade."

She shook her head. "I want to go home." Her voice hitched. "I need to be with Ivy."

He wrapped an arm around her shoulders. "I'll take you right now. How would that be? Maybe we can catch her before bedtime." He was helping her to her feet when he spotted Angela striding toward them, a wool coat wrapped snugly around her.

"I was locking up after my shift at the hospital gift shop and I heard what happened from one of the nurses," she said. Her expression was pained, as if she had swallowed something bitter. "I am so sorry. I can't tell you how bad I feel."

"We'll get Blaze." Angela flinched, and Chad realized his tone was gruff and hard. He tried to temper it. "Have you talked to the police about your own safety?"

She sighed. "Yes. Chief Patron said he'd have an officer drive by on a regular basis to check the grounds when he can spare a man. Tom suggested I hire some private security. I suppose he must be right, but I hate the thought of strangers on my property." A look of hope flitted across her face. "Blaze might flee now, since he's done this terrible thing. Right?"

"Do you think that's likely?" Dory said.

Angela's gaze drifted from Dory's wounded face to the evening sky. "When he was a sixth grader, he had a hard time fitting in at a new school. No friends, though that was probably because of him more than the other kids. Mary signed him up for baseball. He came home from the first practice upset because some other players laughed at him for not knowing how to throw properly. He got a bucket of balls and started practicing, day and night. At all hours, I could hear the whack of that baseball hitting the side of the barn when I stayed over. Whack, whack, all night long." She shook her head. "Do I think he'll give up?" Her gaze locked on Chad. "No, I don't."

Chad instinctively moved closer to Dory. He agreed with Angela. Blaze wasn't going to go anywhere until he got what he wanted.

Angela bent and touched Dory's hand. "Anyway, I just wanted to say that I'm sorry. If only we could have gotten through to Blaze when he was a kid. Maybe if Scott hadn't died so suddenly." The look on her face was pure defeat. "I guess that water's long past the bridge, as my father used to say." She sighed. "I got out my gun last night. Daddy taught me how to shoot. I never in a million years imagined I'd be trying to protect myself from my nephew." After a tired nod, she walked away.

Chad kept a wary eye out as he walked Dory to the truck and they drove to Rock Ridge. Time with Ivy would be healing, he figured, and she'd be under her mother and father's watchful eye. They'd called from the hospital to prepare the Winslows.

Sarah ushered them into the house, looping an arm around Dory's shoulders. Chad saw her lip tremble only once before she plastered on a calming smile. This was the kind of mother who could be counted on. The type who did not run away when the wheels were falling off the wagon. He was glad Dory had a mother like that. When Dory started to sniffle, Sarah drew her into the kitchen. "Give us just a minute, okay?"

"Yes, ma'am."

He found himself alone in the hallway. A creak in the floor snagged his attention and he saw Ivy standing at the bottom of the stairs. The dark shadows made her look small and delicate. She wore a pink unicorn night-gown and clutched a stuffed dog that seemed to be missing an eye. Chad realized she must have sneaked out of bed when she'd heard the front door open. He wondered if she'd caught sight of Dory's condition.

He took a knee. "Hello, Ivy."

"Hi, Daddy."

Daddy. He cleared the sudden clog in his throat. "Did we wake you up?"

"No. I was singing some nighttime songs in my bed. What's wrong with Mommy?"

She had indeed seen the tearful greeting. He chose

his words carefully. "Mommy got hurt. Just a little bit. She's okay."

"Is Grandma taking care of her?"

"Yes." There was probably more he should say, some soothing father words. He didn't know any. She seemed to be mulling it over. He remembered something from Charlie's nighttime rituals. "Uh, how about I tuck you in?"

She didn't answer, just hiked up a fistful of pink nightie and climbed the stairs. He followed her into a room with an impossibly small bed, a night-light that cast moon shapes onto the ceiling, and a box overflowing with plastic animals. On the small wooden table was a pile of Popsicle sticks and a bottle of white glue. He also noted a glass jelly jar filled with what appeared to be Cracker Jack prizes. That gave him a silent chuckle. Dory still had her little collection.

Ivy hopped into bed and he pulled the coverlet up.

"Gonna pray, Daddy?"

"Huh?"

"Mommy always prays when she tucks me in."

"Oh." He felt a flush of anxiety. Praying out loud was not in his wheelhouse. "Well…what does Mommy say?"

She closed her eyes and folded her hands under her chin. "Lord, thank You for this day to live, the mistakes I've made today, forgive. Thank You for the sky of blue. And help me learn to love like You."

Chad found himself staring at this wondrous child whom he had been given the esteemed privilege of parenting. He'd come late to the party and found that his tiny daughter had already learned some lessons he'd been struggling with for years, thanks to Dory.

Forgiveness, love, gratitude.

His eyes were damp and his heart so full he could not make any words come out.

"Now you say the 'Amen' part," Ivy instructed.

"Amen," he whispered, and he meant it with all the fervor of his heart. He pressed a kiss to her forehead.

"Will you tell Mommy I love her?"

"Yes."

"And will you ask Mommy to come lie down with me?"

"Yes."

"And next time can you bring Meatball with you?"

He laughed. "We'll see what we can do. Good night, Ivy."

He had one leg across the threshold when she said it.

"I love you, Daddy."

His insides filled with a light he did not understand. A light that was so much greater than all the dark shadows that lingered deep down. His daughter loved him? This generous, sweet soul could decide so quickly that he was her daddy and that made him worthy of love?

Though he'd only known her for a few days, he knew the truth of it, the depth of it, the power of loving someone whom God had placed squarely in his path for no other reason than because He was so very good. He resolved then and there that, no matter what, he would try with everything in him to be the best father he could possibly be to this little girl.

"I love you, too, Ivy," he whispered before he gently closed the door.

He took the stairs slowly to give his pinballing emotions time to settle. He discovered, to his surprise, that there was a gathering in the living room. Sarah, Pete, Dory and his father.

"Dad?"

Rocky grinned. "When you took our gal to the hospital, I figured me and Pete here could put our heads together." His smile faded. "Time for us to quit squabbling since things have gotten serious."

Pete didn't exactly smile, but his tone was civil. "Blaze is getting desperate. We need to stop him before anything else happens to my daughter."

"Agreed," said Sarah, Rocky and Chad at exactly the same time. Chad took a seat next to Dory at the table. Her eyes were puffy from crying, but she appeared calm and resolute.

A ring of the doorbell announced Danny Patron, who joined them.

"We've got the roads sealed off around town. The bus terminal and the train depot are covered. Blaze isn't going to slip town without our knowing it. Thanks for calling me, Pete. What do you have?"

"I located my computer file, believe it or not," Pete said. "We've been going over the details of the case. We found something interesting." He slid on a pair of reading glasses and thumbed a paper free from the stack. "Here it is, a five-dollar meal fee tacked onto the price of the fishing excursion."

Rocky lifted a shoulder. "I picked up a roast beef sandwich that morning for Blaze, along with a soda. Stored 'em in the cooler while I took care of some stuff. I can't remember clearly, but I assume he ate it."

He paused. "Then I got to thinking about something that always bothered me. Why didn't Blaze swim to shore? Save his mother? Told me he was a good swimmer, though I guess that coulda been a lie, or maybe the waves were too much for him." He cleared his throat.

"If I was intoxicated from something in my thermos, why weren't Blaze and Mary able to swim for help or hold on to something?

"Mary was a tiny thing, but Blaze was a strapping nineteen-year-old kid. He shoulda been able to stay alive until help got there. Both of them were told to wear life jackets, but Mary didn't have hers on when Tom found her."

Chad shifted. "What are you saying?"

"One theory I've been cooking up is that there was something in that sandwich. Maybe Blaze called his Mom to come along and doctored it up when we weren't looking. Drugged her so she couldn't swim properly. Slipped off her life jacket."

"The coroner did a tox screen on Mary," Pete said. "It was inconclusive, but there was a trace of Seconal, which her doctor said he prescribed to help her sleep. It wasn't enough to incapacitate, in his view, but it might have been enough to slow or confuse her."

Dory pressed a hand to her temple. "But there's still the big question… If Blaze's motive was killing his mom for her money, why did he disappear for five years?"

"Could be he really did get a head injury," Pete said. "The water was rough that day with the sudden storm that came up. There was no easy exit point in the direction he was swimming. Or maybe he figured he'd stay away until he made sure there was no question Rocky would be convicted and time got away from him."

Danny frowned. "Okay. Let's play it the other way. Let's say Angela arranged the sinking by doctoring Rocky's thermos and drugging Blaze's sandwich. She didn't know Mary was going to join in. Blaze shared his sandwich with his mom, and they were both incapacitated. Blaze was somehow able to get to shore anyway and save himself. Maybe he realized Angela set up the sinking and panicked, pretended to have drowned, fearful his aunt would try again to kill him."

Dory nodded. "I still don't get it. Angela already has plenty of money. Why would she attempt to murder her nephew for his inheritance?"

Chad was up and pacing. "We already know what kind of person Blaze is. He almost killed Dory."

"But someone shot at us from the bridge, Blaze included," Dory said.

"What if they were both in on it?" Pete held up a hand. "Hear me out. Blaze is tired of waiting for his money. For some reason we aren't privy to, Angela agrees to help him get it by killing Mary and convinces her to join him on the boat. Blaze gives her the drugged sandwich. She drowns after Blaze strips off her life jacket. Blaze is supposedly swept out to sea, scheduled to resurface after Rocky is convicted to claim his money, only Angela double-crosses Blaze and sends people to kill him instead, keeping him on the run for five years."

"Which means," Chad said slowly, "that Blaze and Angela could both be guilty, and now they're desperate to save their skins and hang on to the Robertson money by blaming each other."

Danny's lips thinned into a grim line. "I've heard stranger things. I'll bring Angela in for questioning and see if I can get anything out of her."

Chad grimaced. "We've got to convince Tom that Angela might not be what she seems."

Dory suppressed a yawn but her mother did not miss it.

"Enough for one night," she said. "Time for Dory to rest."

"Ivy asked you to check on her," Chad reported dutifully as he followed Rocky and Danny to the door, letting them exit first before he turned back to Dory. She looked delicate there in the moonlight, as if she was made of something very soft and fragile, though he hoped her spirit was still strong as steel.

On impulse, he pulled her to his chest and kissed the top of her head. This woman, this incredible woman whom he'd despised, had given him the most precious gift he'd ever receive. She'd made him a father. He could not get over it, nor did he want to.

His arms went around her, and as the connection grew between them, he desperately wished it would not end, that they could stay together. Partners in life and in love? The skipping, swirling feeling swept him in and he tipped her face up to meet his. A kiss...just one kiss. His lips barely brushed hers when she scooted a step back. He blinked. What had he been about to do? When she'd made it so clear that he would be Ivy's daddy and nothing more? Right after she'd been battered and almost killed?

"Good night, Chad." Her voice was soft but strong. The message was clear.

"Good night, Dory."

Dory quieted her skittering nerves. She'd almost let Chad kiss her. Somehow she'd found enough strength deep down to prevent what surely would have been a grave mistake. After a breath, she tiptoed into Ivy's room and bent to kiss her.

"Do you feel better?" Ivy said.

"Yes, sweetie." Dory sighed. "I thought you were sleeping."

Ivy pulled a handful of Popsicle sticks from under her pillow. "I'm going to give these to Oliver."

Dory smiled. Oliver was a little boy in her prekindergarten class who had trouble making friends. Mostly he sat by himself and built structures with Popsicle sticks, over and over, again and again, reworking the design until he got it just right. She was proud of her daughter for noticing, for trying to care for Oliver.

"Daddy said maybe Meatball can come visit."

Dory felt a hitch at the word *daddy*. "That would be great. Go to sleep now, Ivy."

"Daddy said he loves me."

A sudden wash of tears blinded her.

"Does he love you, too, Mommy?"

She stood there frozen to the spot. *Does he love you, too?* What could she say to that? He had loved her once upon a time, and though she would give anything to recapture that love, she could not allow him to be yoked into a relationship out of duty. He wanted to be family—that much she knew—and perhaps he might even try to convince himself that he loved her. But she would not ask it of him.

"Go to sleep now, baby," she said, hoping Ivy did not see her tears.

NINETEEN

Dory jolted awake with a pounding headache the next morning. It took her a few moments to calm her juddering heart. Images of Blaze hurling rocks down at her left her breathless. She climbed out of bed and hobbled into the bathroom to swallow two Tylenol. Her face in the mirror horrified her; eyes red rimmed, forehead swollen, skin pale. She was seized by a sudden anger at the man who had stoned her, framed Rocky and possibly killed his mother with or without his aunt's help.

You're a private eye, Dory. Why don't you live up to the name and try to track him down?

Blaze would need help soon. He'd need money, food, shelter or maybe a way to escape town. He'd likely reach out to someone from his past. She decided to focus again on his acquaintances, friends, anyone who might render aid if he called. Throwing on some clothes, she groaned when she remembered her laptop was still in the saddlery. Since it would be foolhardy to travel on her own, she asked her father to ride along with her. She'd drive over quickly and pick it up. Chad would be busy with his morning ranch chores.

Her father was uncharacteristically quiet as they walked to the car.

"What are you thinking about, Dad?"

He shrugged. "Just wondering what Chad's planning to do about Ivy."

She sighed. "I don't know, Dad. Everything's a muddle right now." Ivy's comment scrolled through her memory.

Does he love you, too, Mommy? How beautiful and perfect it would be if she allowed herself to imagine it. She and Chad in love again, raising Ivy as a couple.

Don't do that to yourself. Two weeks ago, she was a committed single mother taking care of herself and her child with no help from Chad. Nothing had changed.

Jamming the key into the ignition, she drove a little too quickly to the ranch. By the time she got to the saddlery, she'd settled her thoughts. Her father stayed on the porch to take a phone call. Letting herself in, she hastily snagged her laptop. A pile of clothes sat on the table, laundered and neatly folded. There was a note on the top.

> *Washed these for you, Dory. Praying for your healing and strength. Love, G.*

On top of the pile were some pieces of metal she didn't recognize at first. In a flash, she was back in that awful cistern, reliving the moment when Blaze hurled the first missile at her. She'd been so shocked and angry, she'd snatched it up and thought about throwing it back until she'd realized the futility of it.

The broken bits were clean-edged, speckled with blue paint. She vaguely remembered he had drawn the objects from his pocket, not picked them up from the ground. When he'd thrown them, they had echoed like metal against the rusted cistern wall.

She fingered the half orb—iron, with a hole drilled in it. Her brain made the identification quickly. It was a broken cable weight.

A memory from the past sizzled to the surface. She was a young teen sitting on an overturned bucket in the boathouse, listening while Rocky had patiently explained.

These little steel balls are fixed to the boathouse cables to hold them straight when the vessels are being lifted in and out of the water.

She remembered the feel of them in her hands; cold metal, smooth, painted a glossy navy blue.

She stared at the metal piece in her palm with a growing certainty.

I know where you're hiding, Blaze.

Though the argument had died away for a moment, Chad's blood was still hot as they raced to the boathouse. He did not dare risk shooting a look in the passenger seat at Dory. Instead he gritted his teeth and tried again.

"I am with your dad on this one. You shouldn't be involved in this."

"Neither should you," she fired back. "The police are going to arrest Blaze."

"I'm going to be an extra set of eyes because he's not going to get away."

"Ditto. Like I told my dad, this is my case and I am going to see it through."

The woman positively infuriated him. Almost stoned

to death and she still insisted on coming. She wiggled a cell phone at him. "Got my phone, and I'll stay in the truck, just like I promised Dad."

"Not good enough."

"It will have to be."

He'd been worrying needlessly about how the trauma of the attack had affected Dory. Her spirit was completely intact. So was her stubborn streak.

The boathouse was a ramshackle structure jutting out over the water. The sides were weathered wood under a rusted red corrugated roof. Overhanging oak trees crowded the rear of the building and dropped acorns and leaves onto the dilapidated rooftop.

Danny Patron was parked behind a grassy hill and suited up in a bulletproof vest, along with two other officers. His face was void of its usual good cheer when he saw Chad's truck pull up.

Chad got out and Dory kept her word by rolling down her window to listen.

Danny jerked his chin at them. "You two are not welcome here."

"We'll stay out of it, but we're gonna be here when you take him down."

Danny's lips thinned. "If you get in the way, I will arrest you. Got me?"

"Yes, sir."

Chad stood next to the passenger's-side door to make sure Dory wasn't going to change her mind. They both watched as Danny and the officers silently moved into position. Danny raised a fist and all three burst into the boathouse.

Chad realized he was holding his breath. The minutes ticked by with no sound. "He's not in there."

Dory groaned. "Maybe I was wrong."

"Or he saw them coming. He could be—" Chad broke off as he saw Blaze appear underneath a nearby pier just as Danny stepped out of the boathouse. Blaze's surprise morphed into a look of fear as he took in the situation and whipped around to retreat.

"He's out here!" Chad yelled.

By the time the fully armed police officers started off in pursuit, Blaze might have already vanished into the thicket of trees that cloaked the inlet. Chad took off, plunging into the shadowy corridor under the pier.

Blaze was fast. Chad pressed harder, his boots digging into the soft dirt. He shot an arm out and grazed the hood of Blaze's sweatshirt. Blaze stumbled but did not go down. Veering away from the water, he beelined toward the trees.

Chad found himself slipping farther behind as he raced across the uneven ground. Blaze broke into the open area between the water and the trees. Maybe Danny's people would catch him there. Chad continued his dogged pursuit, but Blaze was outpacing him. Where was Danny?

A rumbling started up in his ears. From the corner of his eye, he saw his truck lurch into motion, speeding across the mucky earth.

"Dory, stay out of it," he shouted uselessly.

She pressed the gas until the truck flew by him. Her gaze was focused out the windshield, fire in her eyes. Heart in his throat, he watched her press the truck to the max until it drew up next to Blaze. Blaze tried to correct course but there was nowhere for him to go. It was the woods or face Chad and the cops closing in behind. His only hope was to get to the trees before he was caught.

With a roar of engine noise, Dory pulled ahead of Blaze. One foot then two. He could hear the protesting brakes as she abruptly slammed the truck to a stop so quickly it skidded sideways. Blaze smacked into the driver's side and ricocheted backward, tumbling twice until he came to a stop on the wet grass. He struggled to right himself.

"Get away from me," Blaze shouted.

Chad threw himself on Blaze, pinning him in place. "The only place you're going is jail," he grunted as he gripped Blaze's arms behind his back.

One of Danny's officers made it there first, taking over Chad's spot on top of Blaze. Chad stood, panting, and Dory hopped from the truck.

Smiling in triumph, she embraced him. "We got him, didn't we?"

"You got him." He chuckled. "Where'd you learn to drive like that?"

"Morning car pool at school. It's a killer."

He threw his head back and laughed.

The officer was joined by another. They struggled to slip handcuffs on Blaze, who was now screaming and writhing on the ground.

It happened in a flash. He was under control one moment and the next he was leaping to his feet and grabbing for the officer's gun. The cop and Blaze were locked in a lethal wrestling match for control of the weapon.

Chad pushed Dory behind him.

Danny ran toward them.

Blaze's body was rigid with rage as he struggled to remove the gun from the holster. He pulled the weapon clear. Chad stood fast in front of Dory.

A gunshot exploded through the air.

* * *

"Blaze is in surgery." Danny's expression was haggard as he delivered the news to Chad and Dory in the hospital waiting room. "I've never actually shot anyone in my whole career. It's hard to believe it happened."

"I'm so sorry." Dory imagined how difficult it must be for Danny. She'd been second-guessing her own actions, too. If she hadn't insisted on going… If she hadn't pursued in Chad's truck…

Danny waved a weary hand. "It was the right decision. My officers were in danger, so were you and Chad, but, man, it sure feels like a punch in the gut."

Chad blew out a breath. "What's the prognosis?"

"Doc says he's got a good chance if they can control the bleeding. It will be a while before we can get any kind of information out of him."

"At least we know he's not out there able to hurt anyone else for a while," Chad said.

Mitch and Liam arrived in the courtyard. "Sorry for the barking," Liam said. "Jingles and Meatball are in the truck and they are mortally offended to be locked in."

"Situation under control?" Mitch inquired.

Chad filled them in.

"All right," Danny said. "The district attorney's office has someone en route to go over my statement about what happened, but let's have you two down at the station for a proper statement. You'll be talking to another officer who wasn't on scene."

Chad made to follow him.

Dory realized her hands were still clammy with sweat from her nail-biting truck maneuver. "I need to wash my hands. Just be a minute."

Chad nodded and she walked around the corner to

the ladies' room. She tried to make herself believe it was all over, even though they still had no answers. Blaze was in custody. When he recovered, they would finally have the information they sought. The past few hours had proved that Angela had been right. Blaze'd had no intention of giving up.

She thought about the boy Angela had described, hurling a baseball hour after hour. Ruthless. But then she considered Oliver, the little boy in Ivy's school. He built and rebuilt his Popsicle sticks hour after hour, not out of some relentless drive, but because he was a lonely little boy who didn't know what else to do. Making and remaking those structures was his way to have control over the world, to express feelings he could not put into words.

Stick upon stick. Ball after ball.

Had Blaze been that lonely little boy once upon a time? A child who'd turned into something dark and dangerous? The hallway was quiet and deserted, except for a woman with her back to Dory, talking on the phone.

Angela Robertson, Dory realized.

"If he lives, we're going to prison."

The words stopped Dory dead in her tracks. *If he lives? Prison?* She could only be talking about Blaze.

"It was five years ago, Tom," she heard Angela snap. *Tom?*

"We couldn't have known Mary was going to be on that boat. It wasn't our fault. Blaze drove us to it. He deserves to die. You'll have to find a way."

A dull hum started up in Dory's brain as the pieces fell into place. The enormity of her mistake floored her.

Blaze was an angry, dangerous man, but he hadn't been guilty of his mother's death.

It was five years ago, Tom.

Tom Rourke wasn't blindly protecting Angela… He'd been an active participant.

"I know you don't like lying to Chad, but you've done what you could for him. Friendship only goes so far," Angela snapped. "You saved him from your fire, right? He wasn't even seriously hurt. Neither one of them were."

So Tom had set the fire to heap more blame on Blaze? That was why Tom had been there at the perfect moment to save Chad, with a nail conveniently in his pocket. It had all been a colossal setup.

Dory stepped back, but it was too late. Angela swiveled, saw her and lowered the phone.

"So now you know," she said.

Dory tried to force down a swallow. The corridor was isolated. No one would hear her scream. She would turn and run, but before she did so, she had to get the answer to the question that burned in her.

"How did you sink the boat?"

Angela shook her head. She made no move to come closer to Dory or to reach for any kind of a weapon. "Almost the perfect crime, right? Tom spiked Rocky's thermos. Doctored the sandwich for Blaze. He was intending to be on the boat to help things along, but he was delayed. It worked out anyway when the boat overturned. We couldn't have planned it better."

Dory edged back. "Worked out?" She couldn't keep the disgust from her voice. "Your sister died."

What looked like grief pinched the corners of Angela's mouth. "A terrible mistake. We had no idea she'd invited herself along. The wrong person drowned. It should have been Blaze. He didn't get enough of the drug to make him drown. That was the real tragedy."

"Why? Why do you hate him so much, Angela?"

She huffed. "Spoiled brat. He had no right to the Robertson money. My father worked himself to death acquiring that wealth, and Blaze was a no-good, entitled creature from the beginning.

"I tried to tell Mary. I tried, but she insisted on making excuses for him. He never deserved a dime of the family wealth. Ever. Mary changed after he came. She wouldn't listen to me. She defended him over and over again. He could do no wrong in her sight."

Mary had changed, because her child became her priority instead of her sister. "You were jealous of Blaze, weren't you?"

Angela started, eyes narrowing. "Jealous? No, of course not. Mary and I had disagreements over Blaze's behavior, that's all. He was so like his father, lazy, selfish. Mary would have been much better off without him."

Dory shook her head as she backed another step toward the corridor. "So you thought Blaze was drowned like you'd planned, but when you got word that he was alive…you had to kill him."

"I've been trying to find him and kill him for five years," she said grimly.

Dory pulled her cell phone out of her pocket and thumbed it to life. "So Blaze really is innocent."

"He is not innocent. You, above all people, should know that. He almost stoned you to death, remember? Rolled a boulder down on you?"

"Yes, but he didn't kill his mother. You and Tom did."

Fingers closed around her wrist and the phone was yanked away. Tom shoved her against the wall, his forearm across her throat.

"Good thing I was on my way here to pick Angela up." He groaned. "Why couldn't you have left well enough alone, Dory?"

Dory could not free herself or get enough of a breath to scream. Her second mistake. Angela had not disconnected the call. He'd heard everything. He knew that she'd found out. And he'd come to clean up the loose ends.

"You were the one that shot at Blaze at the bridge." She gasped the words out as he pressed her harder to the wall.

Tom sucked in a breath but did not reply.

"All these years. Rocky was your friend. How could you let him go to prison?" Sparks danced in her vision. "And Chad trusts you. They both do."

She felt him flinch, but he didn't let go.

His hands trembled as he held her prisoner. "I started the fire so you'd think Blaze was the bad guy once and for all. That should have been enough to get you off our backs."

She thought about what her father had said. *Seems like we can expunge Tom from the list since he just put his life at risk to save Chad.*

But he hadn't, not really. He'd set the fire, so he'd known all he had to do was go in with the fire extinguisher he'd seen in the hallway, pop the door off its hinges, and he'd be clear of any suspicion.

"That fire almost killed Chad." Blood thrummed in her temples.

"I didn't know it would be like that. I got him out."

There was a stubborn set to his lips. "I can't undo what I've done."

"No," said Angela, "but we can still salvage the situation."

Salvage the situation? Dory started to kick, but Tom turned her around and pressed her face against the wall, cinching her arms behind her.

"Take her out the back exit," Angela said. "There's a side lot that hardly anyone uses. We have to take care of this right now."

TWENTY

Chad gave Dory another minute before he went off in search of her. She'd had a rough ride over some dangerous country the past few weeks and the effects of that were probably going to take a while to catch up with her. Pure exhaustion might explain why she hadn't yet reappeared. Still, when ten minutes ticked away, he went looking for her with no success. Finally, he enlisted the help of a custodian to check the bathroom.

He shrugged. "There's no one in there. Sorry."

Now his nerves were buzzing. Where could she have gone? Was there another restroom he'd missed? He was mulling that over when he noticed the hallway exit door was slightly ajar. Alarm bells jingling in his gut, he jogged over and checked. The door led to a parking lot, empty save for one vehicle. Tom's truck. Odd, since he hadn't seen Tom anywhere in the hospital. He caught a whiff, the barest trickle of fragrance. Something floral and heavy.

And familiar. Angela's perfume.

Angela…and Tom. He felt sick.

He sprinted, phone in hand, filling in his brothers. "I think Angela and Tom may have Dory."

There was no sign of their vehicle. Since the parking lot was wet, he was able to make out the barest hint of tire tracks that indicated a vehicle had recently taken a left out of the lot.

Liam careened up in his truck, sliding over so Chad could drive. The two dogs barked from their crate secured in the bed. He stomped on the gas and peeled out. The frontage road from the hospital was empty. He had only a vague hint since the tracks were rapidly drying. Angela's house was the opposite direction, so they hadn't gone there. Tom lived in the bunkhouse, so that option was out. Where were they taking Dory?

Hands clenching the wheel, he drove the main roads through town, stopping repeatedly to ask if anyone had seen Angela's BMW. No one had. He fought outright panic.

Liam answered his phone, the volume set so loud Chad could hear it was Maggie. Mitch must have alerted the family.

"Got it. Thanks, honey." Liam clicked off. "She just saw a BMW drive past the Lodge, heading for the docks."

The docks. His nerves screamed. Whatever Dory had found out, Angela and Tom were determined she would never divulge it.

Liam's jaw was tight. "So it looks like Tom's in deep."

Chad's mind reeled. How could Tom ever agree to hurting Dory? The man who'd been their friend for decades? The guy who had tried to save Mary Robertson? His blood went cold. Or had he? The notion pierced his gut. He recalled Tom's stricken expression as he'd dragged Mary from the water. Had he been distraught because of the tragedy…or because he and Angela had cooked up a plan to kill Blaze and it had backfired?

The road down to the docks was narrow and damp. As safely as he could, he took the turn, but the rear wheels skidded. Liam didn't comment, but his hand was tight on the armrest. The small parking area was empty save for the crookedly parked BMW. Empty.

"Where's he taken her?" Chad scanned the horizon. He knew Tom owned his own boat, but he couldn't spot it. There were several berths housing a rowboat and two larger vessels. There was no one around anywhere.

The fear was a live thing inside him, clawing to get out. He heard the noise before he saw anything. "There." A small boat with an outboard motor chugged clear of the end of the dock. Tom was at the throttle. Angela stood at the bow, the wind whipping her hair free of the scarf. Where was Dory? Had they killed her? Was she lying bleeding on the decking?

He ignored his brother's shout, tugged off his boots and sprinted to the end of the dock. Tom was goosing the throttle, urging the boat away from the dock, but it took the motor a few precious moments to get up to speed. Chad had only one way of catching Tom and Angela, and he prayed God would give him the strength to carry it out.

Heels pounding hard across the wood slats, he sprinted to the end and threw himself as far out as he could. His stomach somersaulted as he plunged down into the water, a yard off the starboard bow.

Kicking hard, he cleaved the churning waves until he got one hand over the gunwale. The waves cast him loose, but he tried again, struggling to clamp a hand tightly to the boat's side. With a mighty heave, he hauled himself in. Dory was kneeling on the deck, hands and feet bound with duct tape and a strip across her mouth. He read in her wide eyes everything he needed to fuel him. She was alive, scared, and most of all, she believed that he would save her.

He launched himself at Tom, knocking him away from the motor. The boat lurched, finally settling into a violent circling that tumbled them from side to side.

Tom righted himself. His expression was a mixture of anguish and rage. "I didn't want to hurt you or your father."

Chad reeled inside. It was true. He'd been hoping he was wrong somehow, that Tom had not betrayed Chad and his father. "Your words don't mean anything to me," he snarled. "You sent my father to prison and you almost killed Dory. You don't get a pass and you don't get to feel better. You get prison."

"I'm sorry, Chad. I can't go to prison." His punch came so quickly, it almost caught Chad unprepared.

He threw up an arm to deflect it and hooked a left cross that got Tom solidly on the jaw. He went down into the bottom of the boat, dazed. His collapse sent a shock wave through the circling boat, knocking Chad off his feet. Scrambling up, he turned to see Angela with a gun aimed at him, her other hand clutching the side. Dory got up, fear in her eyes.

"I always travel with a gun in my purse," Angela said over the revving motor. "You never know when you'll need it."

"You're not going to get out of this." Chad tried to hold steady against the rocking deck. The boat continued to zoom in dizzying circles. He had to get between Angela and Dory. "Police are already alerted. There's no way out."

Angela considered. "I'll sort it out later, after I get out of here."

Dory was moving closer to the stern and he realized what she meant to do.

Distract Angela or it's all over. "All this killing," Chad said, "and you didn't even need the money. You've got plenty. Why did you do it?"

She pursed her lips. "It's Robertson money. It was never meant to be given to anyone outside the blood-line. Mary should have listened to me. He would have squandered it and then come back for more."

Dory had gotten into position. He swallowed hard, tensed and ready. With one downward chop of her taped hands, she disconnected the fuel line and the boat stopped with a dramatic lurch. The gun flew from Angela's grip into the waves. Chad was flung to his knees. He watched in horror as Dory pitched backward into the ocean.

"No!" he cried. He fought his way to his feet and dived in headfirst, leaving Angela openmouthed on the deck. In the distance, he heard the sound of sirens. A Coast Guard vessel was chugging through the water.

There was no time to wait for rescue. He had to find Dory or she'd drown before help arrived. He swam in helpless circles, scanning the foamy water.

"Dory!" he shouted, but she could not reply, not with her mouth taped. Had she been sucked under the boat? He dived, struggling to see in the agitated waves. A flash caught his attention. The white of her face? Desperately he hauled himself through the water. Despair almost overwhelmed him. *Dory, where are you?* Lungs burning, he dived under again, searching. *There!* She was trapped under the water, her jacket caught in the propeller.

He swam to her, yanked at the zipper. It was hopelessly jammed. He could see panic that mirrored his own flashing in her eyes as she thrashed.

Her eyes begged him.

He prayed. Fury and fear worked together in him. He had to save this woman he loved with a new passion deeper, richer, stronger than anything he'd ever imagined. The cinched zipper refused to let go.

Grabbing hold of the neck of her jacket, he pulled the cloth apart. The ruined jacket floated loose. Yanking her free, he swam to the surface and pulled the tape from her mouth.

She coughed and sucked in choking breaths.

"I got you," he said, looping her bound hands around his neck. He pressed her close. Her body felt so cold next to his. Each and every breath seemed an effort as he trod water for them both.

The Coast Guard pulled near. Angela stood on the rocking deck of the motorboat, her face blank with defeat. All she'd done, all she'd talked Tom into doing, and it was not even to secure money for herself but to keep it from someone she felt wasn't worthy.

He wondered where the Robertson money would go after Angela was sent to prison.

Didn't matter, he thought. The only things that did were the woman in his arms and the little girl waiting at home for them both. Treading water, he rested his cheek against Dory's wet hair and let the rescuers come to them.

Two days later, Dory could not quite believe that she was standing on the Roughwater Ranch, whole and healthy. The spring afternoon was perfect, mild and golden, and there was a sumptuous Opening Day barbecue in progress for anyone remotely connected to Roughwater Ranch and Charlie's baseball team. The smell of charcoal and a crock of baked beans enticed her taste buds. In the distance, she saw Zephyr and Boss nosing the grasses along the fence line.

Uncle Gus helped Jane hang a Let's Play Ball banner above the sliding doors. Inflatable baseball bats decorated the tables. "I never thought we'd be hosting an Opening Day party for fifteen five-year-olds," he laughed.

Mitch laid down a crate holding baseball-themed goody bags. "When does the herd arrive?"

"They're a team, not a herd. You get a half hour more of quiet and then the chaos ensues," Jane said with a grin. "Where is our sporty guy?"

Mitch pointed to the garden. Charlie looked impossibly cute in his baseball uniform following Ivy and Aunt Ginny around the garden.

Danny waved to Dory. He sipped an iced tea and pointed out three young girls in matching yellow dresses. "Those are mine. None of them wanted to play baseball, but we never miss a good party." His smile dimmed and he lowered his voice.

"Tom has confessed to his part in doctoring Rocky's thermos, drugging the sandwich and removing Mary's life jacket. He says everything was his fault. He will not name Angela in anything."

"What?" At her outcry, Chad handed Liam the tongs and left the barbecue he was filling with coals for the hot dog roasting. Danny repeated his information when he joined them.

Chad shook his head. "He's going to defend her to

the end, even though she's the one who cooked up the whole plan."

"We've got enough to convict her anyway. DA's putting everything together and Dory's dad has offered to assist."

Dory nodded. "What about Blaze?"

"When he's released from the hospital, he'll go to jail for his assault on you."

Dory touched Chad's arm. "It's all over." She kept imagining Blaze endlessly throwing that baseball, and she prayed that he would come to someday know about forgiveness and love.

Then there was Tom Rourke. His betrayal would sit heavily on Rocky's soul and Chad's, too. Rocky was now free of the guilt that had mired him, but she knew he would always wonder if he could have done more to save the life of Mary Robertson. She felt the lingering pain of the bruises, latent shivers of fear that rolled over her when she thought of the betrayal they'd endured and the betrayer they had loved. The healing would be slow. None of them would ever fully escape the consequences of what had happened the day *The Second Wind* went down.

Chad looked past her shoulder and chuckled. "Never thought I'd see those three at a family barbecue together."

Rocky sat in the sunlight, chatting with Sarah while he ate chips and salsa. Dory's father stayed close and probably only she noticed his nervous energy. Pete and Rocky were not friends. Likely they might never be, but they were making progress. Ivy's two grandpas, she thought with a start. They'd gone from a tiny family to a sprawling ranchful of pseudo relatives in the space of days. God was good.

"Looks like the world is turning right-side up again," he said softly.

She didn't entirely agree. There was still the muddle to be sorted out of how to fold Chad into her family. "I've been thinking about the calendar, how we can make sure you have enough time with Ivy after we move."

He frowned. "Is that still the plan?"

"Yes." Tension teased her stomach. How could she take Ivy to a different state? But how could she stay when there was no future for her here? They would both grow and change. Since they were not a couple, would she see a new woman in Chad's life someday? Someone he would feel as passionately about as he had her all those years ago? Would Ivy be just one of a brood of children for Chad? When the ache in her heart grew too much to bear, she set the thoughts aside. "Ivy loves the garden."

"She sure does." Chad took her elbow and walked her away from the gathering. "I want to tell you something."

She swallowed. He would probably want to talk more about Ivy, nail down the visitation schedules and trips to the ranch. She couldn't really blame him. In his position, she'd do the same. The only choice was to get it over with as quickly as possible.

Resigned, she allowed him to lead her away.

Chad watched Ivy follow the scampering Meatball through Aunt Ginny's sprawling garden. She and Charlie had been helping Ginny construct a teepee out of slender poles to support the emerging pole beans. He suspected it had taken twice as long with the two kids and one three-legged dog helping, but everyone looked thoroughly satisfied with the outcome. He thought the garden, complete with giggling children and a three-legged dog, was just about the most perfect landscape he'd ever seen. It was only missing one thing.

Dory sighed.

Chad gazed at her profile. Dory Winslow was not the teenager he'd fallen in love with anymore, and he found he was heartily glad about it. She'd become a gracious and forgiving woman who put others first and gave the best of herself to her daughter. Dory lived beautifully, successfully and faithfully in that gray area that Liam had spoken about. Chad hoped with all his might that he had changed, too, from the man who could only see the black and white.

Ivy's prayer echoed in his ears... *Help me learn to love like You.*

Had God grown him up enough to let the past go so he could take on the role of father to Ivy...and husband to Dory? It was time to find out. Swallowing hard, he turned to face her.

"Dory..." But as he looked into her rich honey gaze, all the words fled. He was left silent, motionless and dumbfounded, at the intensity of his thundering emotions. Reaching down, he kissed her gently on the cheek, grazing his lips over the freckled satin.

She let him for a moment, the warmth of their connection spreading before she edged back. "You wanted to tell me something? I've been researching the school calendar dates for Christmas break and long weekends. I..."

He shook his head. "That's not what I want, occasional visits and long weekends. I need something permanent."

She frowned. "Chad, if you're talking about custody…"

"I guess I am, in a way."

Her brow furrowed and she bit her lip.

He blew out a breath. "Let me try again. Yes, I want permanence and custody and everything." He took her hand. "Most of all, I want you, Dory."

Her mouth opened in a surprised circle. "I told you we can work out an arrangement…"

"The only arrangement I want is marriage to you." He'd done it. He'd said it. He stroked her finger. "A ring—my ring, right here."

Her face fell. "I know you want a marriage because you think it's the best for Ivy, but…"

Now he cupped her shoulders and gently shook her. "I want to marry you because there's no one else on this earth I want to spend my life with."

She gaped. "Because I had your daughter?"

"I'm not going to lie. Yes, that's part of it." He would not allow her to look away. "When I see Ivy, I see the best parts of you. I see her joy and love and generosity, and I know she is that way because you are." He struggled to find the words. "Looking at her helps me truly know you. You fill my head and my heart and my spirit, and I love you."

She shook her head. "Oh, Chad. You loved me a long time ago. You're trying to convince yourself of that now because of how you felt when we were teens."

He touched her hair, stroking the soft strands that refused to lie straight. "I love you because of what happened then *and* the five years that followed."

Still, she shook her head. "You only just found out that you're a father. You need more time…"

"We've spent roughly two thousand days apart," he said. "I don't need time. I need you. I love you. I love being with you, Dory. I want to be there every day to see what you're going to become, what we can become together. You, me, Ivy and whoever else God lets us bring into this world."

She'd squirmed out of his grip and gone stone-still, eyes wide, lips apart.

Summoning a deep breath for courage, he called to Ivy. "Hey, pumpkin. Can you bring that box I gave you?"

Ivy raced over with the exuberant Meatball. "Daddy, Polly Pumpkin is doing great in Aunt Ginny's yard. She's got a yellow flower and three new leaves."

"I can see that. We're gonna have the best pumpkin patch in the whole county." He looked in the half-empty Cracker Jack box. "Looks like we're missing some snacks."

Ivy pulled a face. "Meatball was hungry. You said I could share the treats but not the prizes."

He laughed. "I sure did." He handed the box to Dory. "The prize is for your mommy."

Dory's bemusement spoke volumes, but he could not read from her expression how she felt about his proposal. His breath cinched tight as she pulled two tiny pouches from the box while Meatball happily scarfed up the dropped pieces of caramel corn.

"The big prize is for you, Dory."

He watched with a jackhammering heart as she tore open the paper pouch and pulled out the diamond solitaire, the biggest one he could afford. "It's not the one I was going to propose with five years ago because I figured we needed a new start." He dropped to one knee. "Will you take it? Will you marry me? I promise I will never let you and Ivy down."

Tears started to course down her face. "I…"

The other little pouch fell to the ground and Ivy picked it up. "What's this one, Daddy?"

"That one's for you."

She opened it and held up the little gold pumpkin charm with three initials on the back. *D* plus *C* plus *I*. "It's for me?" she squealed.

"Yes, ma'am. To remind you that we're a family." He turned to Dory. "I haven't heard your answer. Will you marry me, Dory Winslow? I'll live in Arizona if that's what you want. Or we can make a home here. Whichever you think is best for Ivy."

She was still blinking, but now he saw tears in her eyes. It was not enough. He'd not convinced her. He felt the blow deep in his core. "I…I love you," he repeated. "All I want in the world is to marry you."

And then she was smiling. That smile held his future, their future, struggles, triumphs, hopes and dreams. A glorious electricity raced up his spine.

"Yes," she whispered. "I love you, Chad. I love you so much."

He swooped her up and swung her into a circle. "Ivy, your mommy is going to marry me. What do you think of that?"

Ivy laughed. "Hip, hip, hooray!" she said.

"That's for certain. Hip, hip, hooray!" he shouted. "Dory's gonna marry me."

That earned a joyful whoop from the family collected on the porch. From the corner of his eye, he saw

Rocky shaking Pete's hand. The world blurred until all that remained was their tiny family, haloed in the golden spring sunlight. He buried his head in Dory's neck to hide his sudden tears.

Meatball yipped at the family commotion.

Dory laughed. "I don't think Ivy will settle for leaving Meatball out of the family."

Chad threw back his head and guffawed. "Of course not. That dog is going to be her best friend ever. He's Meatball Winslow Jaggert, after all." He kissed her then, long and slow, and reveled in the wonder of his long-ago family, born anew.

* * * * *

*If you enjoyed this story,
look for the other books in the
Roughwater Ranch Cowboys series:*

Danger on the Ranch
Deadly Christmas Pretense
Cold Case Connection

Dear Reader,

Life is messy, isn't it? I am typing this in the days following the loss of our beloved Grandpa Mentink, a fantastic man who enjoyed sixty-nine years of marriage to an exceptional lady. Listening to the stories of their years together reminds me how precious love is and how dear families are. God knows how difficult the days can be here on planet Earth, and He places people in our lives to help us along each treacherous mile. I witnessed many of those dear people coming forward during the funeral preparations to assist and comfort in every way possible. Each and every one of them was a blessing to our Mentink family.

In this novel, Chad and Dory are going to get a second chance to repair their family and let go of the anger and resentment that has torn them apart. Of course, reconciliation is so much easier in fiction than in real life, but it is my hope that each one of you knows what unconditional love and forgiveness feel like.

God bless you, my friends, and thanks for coming along on this journey with me. As always, if you'd like to contact me, you can send a message via my website at www.danamentink.com. There is also a physical address listed there.

Hugs and much love,

Dana Mentink

WE HOPE YOU ENJOYED
THIS BOOK FROM

LOVE INSPIRED SUSPENSE
INSPIRATIONAL ROMANCE

Courage. Danger. Faith.

Find strength and determination in stories
of faith and love in the face of danger.

6 NEW BOOKS AVAILABLE EVERY MONTH!

"Willa!" Olivia's horrified gasp indicated she knew the woman was gone. "Oh, no! Where's Aaron?"

"Olivia, please," he tried but then he heard the sound of someone coming down the stairs. "Run away and call for help."

"Not without my son!"

"Go!" He pushed Olivia toward the door then quickly but silently crossed the living room into the kitchen, flipping the light off as he went. There was a side doorway that he felt certain led up to the second-story apartment.

He took up a defensive position behind the door and waited, hoping the guy who likely had Aaron didn't know that his cohort in crime had failed at kidnapping Olivia.

"Mommy! Mommy! I want my mommy!" Aaron's cries echoed high and shrill above the thumping footsteps coming down the stairs.

"Aaron! I'm here, baby, don't worry!" Olivia's voice rang out loudly and Ryker momentarily closed his eyes, wishing he'd handled things differently.

He should have gotten Olivia and Aaron out of the city the moment he'd found them.

Instead he may have caused the very thing he'd been trying to avoid.

Getting them both killed.

Don't miss
Guarded by the Soldier *by Laura Scott,*
available July 2020 wherever
Love Inspired Suspense books and ebooks are sold.

LoveInspired.com

Get 4 FREE REWARDS!

We'll send you 2 FREE Books plus 2 FREE Mystery Gifts.

Love Inspired Suspense books showcase how courage and optimism unite in stories of faith and love in the face of danger.

FREE
Value Over
$20